MAYA AND THE ROBOT

by **Eve L. Ewing**

illustrated by
Christine Almeda

Kokila

Kokila
An imprint of Penguin Random House LLC, New York

First published in the United States of America by Kokila,
an imprint of Penguin Random House LLC, 2021

Text copyright © 2021 by Eve L. Ewing
Illustrations copyright © 2021 by Christine Almeda

Visit us online at penguinrandomhouse.com.

Library of Congress Cataloging-in-Publication Data is available.

Book manufactured in the United States of America

ISBN 9781984814630

2 3 4 5 6 7 8 9 10
LSC

Design by Jasmin Rubero
Text set in Modum Family

This book is dedicated to anybody

looking for a friend.

–E. L. E

CHAPTER 1:
THE WORST SCIENCE FAIR EVER

If you looked outside through the cafeteria windows, it seemed like a perfectly normal day. The sun was shining. Birds were chirping. A regular day. A *beautiful* day, even. But inside the cafeteria, things were anything but normal. All around me, kids and adults were screaming. I tried to shut out the chaos for a second and focus on the sunlight. *Just breathe,* I told myself. *Count your breaths. Calm down. One ... two ...*

"Yaaaaarghhhh!" came the ear-piercing yell from behind me. "My computer is covered in pudding! Pudding!"

I spun around to see Zoe Winters, the most popular girl in my class, standing in front of a display table where her science fair project had once stood. When I had walked into the cafeteria carrying my own project, I'd noticed how neat the whole thing was—the letters that spelled the project title, "Coding and Circuits," across the top of the board, the computer and circuits and batteries set up in a display at the front of the table.

Now it was a mess that mostly resembled a pudding waterfall. Pudding dripped over the title, smeared across the letters so it said COD CIRCU S. Pudding filled the keys of the computer keyboard. But I really cringed when I saw something even worse than ruining an expensive computer. Zoe hadn't noticed yet, but there was also—

"PUDDING IN MY HAIR! CHOCOLATE PUDDING IN MY HAIR!"

Okay. I guess she had noticed. Brown, thick, fudgy droplets cascaded from Zoe's once-perfect curls into her eyes, and she stopped saying words and started making horrible gurgly sounds. "Ayyyaaazzzrrrruuuggghhhmaaargh!"

I was going to go over and help her when a streak of something yellow flew past my ear. I looked behind

me to see that it was creamed corn. It had been launched with the accuracy of a fastball, landing dead center in a huddle of screeching first graders. They were sheltering in the corner with their teacher, screeching and giggling at the pudding waterfall, but now that it was raining corn, they started panicking and running in circles, except for one kid who must have been hungry, because he started trying to catch the bits of flying corn with his mouth.

"Mommy, I don't like corn!" wailed a kindergartner. She took off running at top speed to try to get as far away from the corn hurricane as possible. "No, stop!" I yelled after her, but it was too late. She skidded on a gross mixture of pudding and corn that was waiting on the floor like a cartoon banana peel, her light-up gym shoes slipping and sliding as she struggled to stay upright. Desperate, she grabbed the nearest solid piece of furniture—the corner of the display table where my best friend Jada was trying to guard the scale model she had built of a suspension bridge. It was a work of art. I could tell Jada must have fussed over it for weeks—it wasn't any old thing she made out of a kit. There were LEGOs and toothpicks, tiny wires, plastic beads, Popsicle sticks, and even a tiny glowing LED light at the top of the bridge. It was complex and beautiful. The little kid grabbed the table, and Jada froze, seeing her creation in danger but not knowing what to do. She couldn't push a younger kid out of the way, but I could see by the pain in her face that she was strongly considering it. "Noooooo!" a voice screamed, and when they both turned their eyes on me I realized that the voice was mine.

Have you ever seen one of those videos that shows an avalanche coming down a mountain in slow motion? Imagine that, but replace the snow with LEGOs and toothpicks and beads, and you'll see what I saw as Jada's project came tumbling down onto the small girl sitting pitifully on the floor in a puddle of pudding.

Jada stood there, arms hanging at her sides, and watched it happen. For a second she seemed to be in shock. Then she took a deep breath, furrowed her brow, and hollered at the top of her lungs: "THIS! IS THE WORST! SCIENCE FAIR! EVERRRR!" And then she began to cry. First her voice, then her sobs, reverberated around the room, but no one seemed to hear her. Everyone was too busy trying to handle the disaster that was unfolding.

The gym teacher was blowing his whistle for order. But it stopped making any sound when a blob of mashed potatoes flew into his face. He kept blowing, but the whistle only shot out white specks of mashed potatoes with every breath. Ms. Hixon, the cafeteria lady, had transformed into some kind of acrobatic martial artist, leaping from table to table, slapping flying food projectiles out of the air with a huge metal spoon. "You think this is my first food fight? This ain't my first food fight!" she yelled at no one. In one corner, there was so much creamed corn spilled on the floor that it made a pond large enough for several preschool kids to be sitting in it and having the time of their lives, putting it in each other's hair and throwing it at each other and grinning like it was a playground sandbox. Near the door, Mr. Samuels, the custodian, was standing forlornly with a bucket, shaking his head. "Nope," he said over and over. "Nope, nope, nope. No way. I'm gonna need a bigger mop." Pudding and mashed potatoes and corn were on *everything*. On the tables, the floors, the walls, in people's hair. Pudding was splattered on the windows. People were digging mashed potatoes out of their ears and wiping it off their glasses.

And smack dab in the middle of the mayhem, there he was. Whirling in circles at top speed, scooping food out of industrial-sized vats and launching it in every direction. Beeping at a terrible high pitch, flashing multicolored lights, and appearing perfectly willing to spend the whole rest of the day tossing potatoes at people with no sign of stopping. This calamity, the screaming, the mess, the ruined science fair ... this was his fault.

No, I realized. This was *my* fault.

After all, he was my robot.

My spinning, beeping, flashing, food-catapulting, going-completely-berserk-in-the-school-cafeteria robot.

Right on cue, I felt a tap on my shoulder and turned around to see Principal Merriweather. She was scowling. I gulped.

"You, my dear, are in big, big trouble," she said.

I opened my mouth to respond, but before I could speak, a glob of pudding hit me right in the middle of my forehead.

I guess I kind of deserved that. And I found out that getting hit in the head with projectile pudding is more painful than it looks.

How did I get here? I didn't wake up, hop out of bed, and say, "I want to be a troublemaker kid who brings a robot to school and stands by doing nothing while it goes bonkers in the cafeteria, starts a creamed corn apocalypse, ruins the science fair, and makes my best friend cry." Definitely not my goal. I swear, I'm really a regular person. And at the moment, a regular person who is probably about to get suspended, unless for some reason the principal *enjoys* wearing a pile of mashed potatoes as a hat.

Well . . . I'm a *mostly* regular person. A regular person with a robot.

But it wasn't always that way. If the year had gone how I'd wanted it to, I probably wouldn't have a robot at all.

It all started on the first day of school.

CHAPTER 2:
THE FIRST DAY

Pancakes. Warm, golden, perfect pancakes. Thousands of them, piled high. A *mountain* of pancakes. I put on my climbing gear, threw my rope and grappling hook up Pancake Mountain, and started to make my way toward the summit. As I went along, I reached out and grabbed pieces of the mountain and popped them into my mouth. Glistening streams of maple syrup flowed down the side, and I stuck my tongue out to catch the droplets of sweetness. Then, in a booming voice, someone was calling to me from the peak. What's that they were saying? They seemed upset. Who could be upset on Pancake Mountain?! Pancake Mountain is a place of joy and happiness. Who—

"MAAAAYAAAAAAAA! I AM NOT! GOING TO

TELL YOU! AGAIN! Turn that alarm off and let's get a move on!"

I sat straight up in bed and rubbed my eyes. I looked around. Not a pancake to be found. Not even the mini-size silver dollar ones. And my mom, from the sound of things, was not happy. It would be so nice to just drift back to sleep, where everything was cozy and warm and syrupy. If only I could turn off that alarm.

My eyes darted to the corner of the bedroom I share with my little brother, Amir. On the desk was a bunch of dried Play-Doh he had left out, a couple of stuffed animals, a model of the solar system with little teeth marks in Saturn and Mercury (I mentioned the little brother, right?), a pile of my overdue library books (I'm almost done with that Mae Jemison biography, and then I'll send it back! I swear!), and the beeping alarm clock. Next to it was . . . my book bag full of school supplies and the clothes I had laid out the night before. *Oh my gosh. Today is the—*

"First! Day! Of! School!" The bedroom door flew

open and my mother leaped into the room. She tugged the covers off of me.

"Let's go, Patricia Maya Robinson!" My mother has two jobs but somehow manages to have the most enthusiasm and energy of anyone in the world. I knew she had been up before the sun, getting Amir ready for my grandma to pick him up and take him to day care, getting my lunch together, and listening to the radio. Unlike pretty much every other adult I've ever met, she didn't even drink coffee, but she always seemed ready to do backflips in the morning. *Maybe that would be a good science fair project,* I thought. *Adult responses to caffeine. Does it have to do with age? Height? Weight? Blood type? What about—*

"Maya, don't make me tell you again."

"I got it, Mom. I'm up." I groaned and climbed out of bed. "I'll get dressed."

"Oh, I know you will," she replied. She went over to the desk, threw the dried Play-Doh in the trash with lightning speed, and picked up the neatly folded school clothes. She tossed them onto the foot of the bed. "You got five minutes, baby girl. I need you washed, dressed, and ready to eat, fast, so you can get out the door on time. I picked up Ms. Yolanda's shift, and I can't take you to school if you miss the bus."

"Okay," I mumbled, still half-asleep. Drowsily, I tugged off the satin bonnet that I had worn to protect my freshly braided first-day-of-school hair. I was surprised it stayed on throughout all my sleeping and dreaming. I probably had a big line on my forehead.

"Better hurry up," Mom called over her shoulder as she hustled out of the room and back to the kitchen. "I made pancakes."

"Pancakes!" Suddenly I wasn't so sleepy. "Why didn't you say so?"

I got dressed in record time.

If only the first day of school had ended as well as it started. The pancakes were delicious, and then it was pretty much downhill from there.

When got to the playground, right away I headed to where MJ and Jada would be waiting for me. I know everyone thinks that their best friends are the *best* best friends, but my friends are the certified, record-breaking greatest friends in the solar system. Probably the galaxy. I was really excited to get back to school and see them. Most of the kids at my school live in different neighborhoods and different parts of the city, so I don't get to see them as much as I want to. Sometimes I read books and see TV shows where the characters are riding bikes to each other's houses every day after school, and that always makes me sort of jealous. If I could ride my bike to see Jada or MJ, I would be with them twenty-four hours a day, seven days a week. Instead, I have to wait for someone to plan it out and give me a ride. That's no fun.

When we are able to get together, we think of really creative things to do. Jada and MJ are always down to assist with my latest science project, and they get just as excited as I do when I can actually get something to work. One time we spent twelve hours building a Rube Goldberg machine that could tip a watering can and water a plant when you put a race car on a track. Another time we made up our own movie, with a script and everything, and then MJ's brother let us use his phone to record it and edit it. It was a mystery called *The Case of the Missing Toaster*, and I got to be the detective searching for the toaster, MJ was the villain who stole it, and Jada was the director. We tried to make MJ's cousin Boogie play the role of the toaster, but he wouldn't do it. Another time we went down to Jada's basement, built a giant fort out of blankets, and spent the rest of the day with some flashlights, making up stories and looking through the photos and yearbooks Jada's grandpa left down there, laughing at the funny old hairstyles and fashions. Jada's mom has a catering business, and sometimes she lets us help her prepare food for someone's birthday or wedding shower. One time she showed us how to test if a cupcake is done (you stick a toothpick in the center, and if it comes out wet, it needs more time) and how to perfectly balance a cherry on top of a bunch of frosting.

On Halloween, sometimes we trick-or-treat at MJ's because he lives in a really big apartment building with hundreds of people, not just three apartments like my building. Last year we went door to door inside, which was good because it was pouring rain out, and we still got a lot of candy. I knew that this year we could have just as much fun. When we hang out at my house, we usually play with Amir, and since I have the biggest LEGO collection of anybody, we work on those for hours and hours, either following directions or making our own LEGO designs. We don't have to be super creative all the time. Sometimes we play video games or watch television and relax. Daddy calls us the Three Jedi Knights. He's the one who showed us the original Star Wars movies, and then he showed us the old cowboy Westerns where George Lucas got his ideas from. Some people would laugh if they went to visit their friend and their friend's dad wanted to watch a bunch of old movies, but Jada and MJ were completely into it. They're really open to trying something new, and even if they weren't feeling it, they wouldn't have laughed. See what I mean? Greatest friends in the Milky Way.

I spotted them right away, in our usual spot by

the fence, overlooking the basketball court. MJ and I are into watching on the sidelines. Jada, who is a basketball fiend, wishes she could jump in the game. But the older kids always take over, and so Jada usually lingers at the edge of the fence with lost-puppy-dog eyes, trying to get up the courage to ask them if she can join.

Today was no different. "I can't wait until we're in seventh grade," she said when I arrived. No hello or anything, and she didn't look at me directly. Her eyes were locked onto the ball as it bounced three times against the pavement and then soared through the air, arcing toward the basket. "As soon as I get a chance, I'm—"

"Gonna be the first in line for tryouts," MJ said. We've heard this speech so many times that he's able to finish the sentence for her at this point. Jada barely noticed, still hypnotized by the action on the court.

"Didn't Coach Tanaka say she might let you try out next year?" I said to Jada, poking her gently in the arm to remind her that MJ and I exist. "Since you're already as tall as most of the seventh-grade girls anyway."

"Yeah," Jada said wistfully. She turned, consciously noticing me for the first time. "Hi, Maya."

"Hi, Jada! Hey, MJ!"

Before MJ could respond, an older boy who overheard us walked away from the court and leaned over the fence, furrowing his brow. MJ rolled his eyes. He already knew what was coming.

"Ay!" said the boy. "I got a question. If your name is Michael Jordan, why you so scrawny?" MJ ignored him. But Jada wasn't here for it.

"*First* of all," she said, stepping up to the fence to face the boy. "Your joke isn't very original. He's heard it a million times. 'Ooh, let's see a dunk, Michael Jordan.' 'Where's your championship ring, Michael Jordan?' It's old. Second of all, our boy here grew a good two inches over the summer! Can't you tell? Sure, okay, some of that is his hair standing up, but—"

By this point, Jada had managed to bore the older boy to death, and he lost interest in making fun of MJ, wandering back toward the action of the game. MJ was flushed red, ready to about die of embarrassment.

"Man, you gotta ignore them," Jada said. "We're in fifth grade now. Forget their old jokes."

"And you really *did* grow some over the summer," I said. As MJ stood there with his arms crossed, fuming, I walked around him so that we were standing back-to-back. We were about the same height, but I hovered my hand over both of our heads so that it was hard to tell who was taller. "See? You're taller than me!" MJ was unconvinced.

"I wish I didn't *have* to ignore them," he said, frowning. "Why couldn't I have a regular name? Even *Michael* without the *Jordan* would be an improvement. I don't know what my dad was thinking."

"He was thinking you was gonna be great!" said Jada. "Epic. Unstoppable. A high school basketball star, following in the footsteps of his pops." She folded her arms, pretending to cradle a baby, and batted her eyes down lovingly. "He was looking at you, his brand-new baby boy, and thinking, *He is going to be exactly what it says on the statue.* 'The best there ever was. The best there ever will be.'"

Last year, MJ's dad had taken the three of us to our first basketball game. His brother, MJ's uncle, works for the city, fixing big potholes in the ground. His job gave him free tickets for a special occasion, and we got to go. We sat so way up high that the players were the size of hamsters as they ran around on the court, but it was still one of the best days ever. And we took a picture together in front of the big Michael Jordan statue. *The best there ever was. The best there ever will be.* Ever since then, Jada had become obsessed with the phrase, writing it in the back of her notebook over and over.

She turned and grinned at me. "You finally made it!" she said. "I was worried you would be late for the first day of school." She gave me a big hug. Jada is the kindest person I know. A lot of kids act scared of her or think she's mean because she's so much taller than them, but she has been my friend and stuck by me since we were in kindergarten, and she helped me get the best blocks off of the top shelf that I couldn't reach. But it's not because she's my bestie—she's nice to everybody.

I stepped back and lifted a hand to greet MJ, since that older boy had interrupted us. "Hey, grumpy."

MJ reached a hand out, and we exchanged our special dap. Two quick slides of the hands, two quick taps of a peace sign against our chests, and an exploding fist. "Hey, goofy," he said back. This was our ongoing joke. MJ is as kind-hearted as Jada. But he's not so quick to show it. He's always got this super-serious frowny face, and his brain tends to jump to thinking about the worst thing that could possibly happen. He says that I'm too quick to lose track of things, to let my mind wander and start thinking about impossible stuff instead of facing reality. I say that he's too negative, always so concerned about the bad things that could *maybe* happen that he forgets the good stuff that *is* happening. Maybe we're both right, and that's part of what makes us a good match as friends—not being the same, but being two sides of the same coin.

I reached into my pocket, grabbed the small

plastic bag of apple slices I had brought with me from home, and started to munch on one. "So, are y'all feeling ready for today? I'm just the teeniest bit scared. I know I'm ready for fifth grade, but I have heard that Ms. Rodríguez is really mean and strict."

Jada and MJ both gave me a funny look that made me nervous. Was I being a baby? "I mean, don't get me wrong," I said quickly. "I think we can handle it together. And this is the science fair year! Just kinda got butterflies in my stomach is all."

They looked at each other, then back at me. "Maya," said Jada gently. "We both got letters last

week saying that we're gonna be in Ms. Montgomery's class." She furrowed her brow, worried about me. "We assumed you got a letter too."

Ms. Montgomery? They were in Ms. Montgomery's class?

"What do you mean?" I understood what they were saying but also didn't get it at all. MJ, Jada, and I had been in the same class since we were five years old. Being in school without them was . . . well, I couldn't even imagine it.

"I guess some new kids transferred into the school at the very end of the summer, and they had to switch some things around to make the numbers work. MJ and I ended up with Ms. Montgomery."

Ms. Montgomery had a reputation for being the coolest, most fun teacher in the entire school. She played the blues guitar in a band on the weekends and sometimes would bring it to school and sing songs. She had three dogs, and her room was decorated with pictures of them and lots of other animals. And, most important to me, she was a scientist. A real one. She had been a chemist before becoming a teacher, and she was always showing off amazing science demos in her class. She was even friends with some of the people at the Museum of Science and Industry, and when she took her classes on field trips there, they got special behind-the-scenes tours.

MJ and Jada were going to be in Ms. Montgomery's class listening to her play guitar and sing songs she made up about the water cycle and the different parts of the ecosystem, and doing real lab experiments with microscopes and chemicals. Meanwhile I would be stuck in Ms. Rodríguez's class. Ms. Rodríguez, whose main claim to fame was that she once made a kid write a ten-page report about gum after he stuck some under a desk. Great.

And worst of all, we wouldn't be together. How would I make friends? Who would I sit with at lunchtime? Who would I do group projects with?

Instead of asking any of these questions out loud, I stood there in silence, feeling like a rain cloud was hovering over my head. My worry must have shown on my face, because MJ reached out and patted me on the shoulder. "It'll be okay, Maya," he said. "Even if you don't make any new friends, there's always next year."

"Next year?!" Jada gave him a look. "Don't listen to him, Maya. You're going to have a *great* year. And we can still hang out in the morning. We might have recess at the same time, too! Plus, how bad can Ms. Rodríguez really be?"

I was about to try to say something brave, when we were interrupted by an ear-shattering whistle. We looked toward the school entrance. Ms. Montgomery was standing by the door. She had long dreadlocks elegantly twisted up on the top of her head, a huge pair of glasses with gold rims, and she was holding a bright-pink clipboard. Students were crowding around her eagerly, and she was greeting each of them with a warm smile.

But she was not the one who had blown the whistle.

"Fifth grade!" bellowed a woman standing nearby. "Fifth grade, it's time to line up! Immediately!" She looked around the playground, scowling. She stood at attention, her back completely straight, and she held a regular plain-looking brown clipboard in her hand, which she tapped impatiently. She reminded me of Miss Trunchbull from the book *Matilda* by Roald Dahl. Across the playground, kids were scurrying over to her, terrified to get caught in her glare.

This was Ms. Rodríguez.

Jada gulped so loud that I could hear her from a few inches away. Then she smiled a thin smile, putting on a positive face for my benefit. "Well . . ." she said. "Let's go line up! Maybe we'll see you later today, Maya."

"Yeah," I said weakly. "Maybe." MJ started to say something but obviously couldn't come up with anything, so he made a weird face, baring his teeth at me. Clearly, it was supposed to be a smile, but MJ is not very good at faking his emotions.

"Uh . . ." he said awkwardly. "Enjoy . . . your . . . um . . . Don't forget to write down your homework assignments at the end of the day!" And he sprinted off, lining up with his class. I nodded and started walking toward the door. I knew that I was walking to my doom.

CHAPTER 3:
THE PERFECT FRIEND

When I got home from school, I went straight to my room, threw my book bag on the floor, and flopped onto the bed. What a day.

Ms. Rodríguez had somehow managed to be even worse than I expected. Her room was arranged with the desks in rows and columns so that everyone sat by themselves, in alphabetical order. When she talked, she barked out commands. Most of the time when she asked a question everyone was too afraid to raise their hands, so she called on people at random, which is how I found myself messing things up with her almost instantly.

"And what do we know about multiplying numbers by zero?" she asked the class during the math period, tapping a yardstick impatiently against the ledge of the chalkboard. "Anyone? Anyone?" I scribbled in my notebook, hoping that maybe if I didn't look at her I would turn invisible. Except there was nothing to take notes on at that moment, so I was drawing the same tiny circles and lines over and over. No one else volunteered an answer, either. Ms. Rodríguez picked up her clipboard and looked at the attendance sheet. "Let's hear an answer from . . ." She ran her fingertip down the line. "Patricia?" I gulped and looked up. Everyone looked around the room. Most people looked at me, knowing that Patricia is my real first name. I was named after my grandma as a sign of respect, but I've always gone by my middle name, Maya. A couple of the new kids and kids I didn't know that well turned their heads back and forth, confused, wondering who "Patricia" was.

I didn't know what to do. Usually, this was the point where I would nicely correct someone about my name. My mom and dad had taught me a certain polite way to do it. "Actually," I would say, "I prefer to go by my middle name, Maya." And then I would answer the question. The *prefer* part made it sound very grown-up and responsible and polite even though I was correcting someone.

But in that moment, Ms. Rodríguez was staring at me with this scowl on her face, and I don't know why, but I completely froze. "Patricia?" she repeated. "Aren't you Patricia?"

"Um . . . I . . ." Before I could put a sentence together, Zoe Winters spoke up, loudly. Even though no one was even talking to her. "Yes, Ms. Rodríguez," she said in her most overly dramatic voice. "That's Patricia Robinson." I shot her a look. Like, *Thanks, I think I remember my own name.* Except, in that moment, I guess I didn't.

"Okay, Ms. Patricia Robinson," said Ms. Rodríguez. "Let's hear it. What happens when you multiply numbers by zero?"

Everyone was looking at me, and I didn't like it. I wished a huge snow cloud could appear out of nowhere and drop an instant blizzard on our heads so that everyone would freeze and be covered with snow. Or maybe an alien spaceship could land on the playground, so everyone would run to the window to see it and forget about me altogether. Anything to get me out of this situation. But no magical blizzard or alien invasion appeared, and I felt my cheeks getting hot as everyone waited for me to respond. I could sense that my classmates were grateful—as long as Ms. Rodríguez was focused on me, they were spared. Finally, I managed to say a few words, quietly.

"When you multiply—" My voice squeaked like an old rusty bicycle. I cleared my throat and tried again. "When you multiply a number by one—I mean zero—it equals zero. Zero times anything is always zero."

"Zero, zero, zero," Zoe repeated in a whisper behind me. No one else seemed to hear her. I couldn't tell if she was making fun of me or not, but somehow it made me feel even worse.

"That's right," said Ms. Rodríguez. "Thank you, Patricia." I winced. Here it was, another chance to make things right. If I could speak up . . . For a second I felt time slowing down. Has that ever happened to you? I've felt that way before, when I'm embarrassed or when things feel out of control. A voice in my head was yelling at me. *Speak up! This is your chance! Now! Go, go, go!*

But all I did was nod. I didn't say a word. And then, time was moving at a regular speed again, and Ms. Rodríguez moved on to something else. I nervously tapped my pencil against the side of my desk, feeling terrible. After a few minutes, I tapped it so hard that I dropped it, and it rolled behind me and toward Zoe's desk. She picked it up and handed it back to me. Just before I took it, she smirked. "Here you go, *Patricia*," she said, showing a toothy great white shark smile.

I tried to remember Jada's words. *Ignore them.* I took it. "Thanks."

I couldn't wait until recess, when I would have a chance to talk it over with my friends. Even though I had said the right answer to the math question, I felt so small in the moment, and embarrassed. I hadn't done anything wrong, but I felt sick to my stomach. And I felt ashamed that I had failed to correct Ms. Rodríguez about my name. *Your name is sacred,* my grandma always told me. *It belongs to you. You have to protect it.* I wanted to see a familiar face, someone to remind me that I was still Maya and to make me laugh or distract me.

So I was disappointed when I got to the playground and saw that Jada and MJ weren't there. Their whole class was still inside. As my classmates ran to the swings and formed circles, laughing and talking, I found Principal Merriweather, who was monitoring the playground. "Excuse me," I asked, "do you know where Ms. Montgomery's class is?" Principal Merriweather looked down at me. She was a tall, thin woman with gentle eyes. She had been born in Mississippi, which came through in her soft southern accent. "Hello, Maya," she said. "How are you? How is your first day going?"

"It's okay," I lied. "But do you know where—"

"Aha," she interrupted me, and I saw a moment of understanding in her face. "You are looking for Ms. Montgomery's class. Because you want to see MJ and Jada, don't you?"

Could she read my thoughts? I nodded at her, feeling confused. "Well," she continued, "I'm afraid they're not here, honey. They have the second recess break, at eleven o'clock."

"A different recess?!" My mouth fell open. Eleven o'clock? *You've got to be kidding me.* Not only was I not going to see MJ and Jada right now, I wasn't going to have recess with them ever. Ever. For the whole year. As Principal Merriweather gazed at me calmly, I looked desperately over the playground. Who was I going to talk to? Who would play with me? Listen to my bad jokes? Make me feel better about having the meanest teacher in the whole world? My face started feeling hot again, and my eyes stung. I swallowed. No way was I going to cry. Not on the first day of school. Not in front of the principal. Not a chance. Not—

"Oh, my dear." Principal Merriweather reached out and put an arm around me as tears fell down my face. "I know it's hard to have new routines," she said. "And to meet new people. I understand you wanted to be in a class with your friends. But it's going to be okay." I pulled away from her, wiping my face on my sleeve. I understood what she was saying, but I could barely hear her. I was so mortified at having cried on the playground. In fifth grade! Who does that? My eyes darted over to the swings. I hoped no one had seen me. I took a step back from Principal Merriweather and coughed.

"It's okay," I said. "I'll be okay. Thanks." And before she could say another word, I was gone. I spent recess in the familiar corner by the fence, kicking a chunk of cement around with my shoe and pretending I didn't care.

The next day was more of the same. And the next. And the one after that. By Friday afternoon, as I lay on my bed remembering the whole week, I felt defeated. On Monday I would have to go back to school with a teacher who called me by the wrong name and no hope of even seeing my friends for more than a few minutes. There had to be something I could do. Something to make the days better, to make a new friend who could stick by me and see me through this year. There was no way I could make it alone.

Amir was on the floor, singing happily to himself as he stacked blocks into a tall column. I leaned over the edge of the bed and poked him on the shoulder. He grinned his baby grin.

"Amir, what would you do if you were having a hard time at school? And your teacher was mean to you?"

He furrowed his brow for a second like he was trying very hard to understand what I was saying, then nodded and pointed at his blocks. "Block, Maya. Block! Maya have block?"

"No thanks," I said gloomily.

"Maya have block!" He threw a block at my arm and giggled as it bounced onto the floor.

"Ow. We don't throw, Amir. No throwing."

He nodded seriously and went back to what he was doing. I sighed. One day Amir would be old enough for me to talk to when I was feeling lonely, but today was not that day. I frowned and looked at the red mark on my arm where the block had hit me. Ouch. Staring at the ceiling, I felt my mind start to wander. *The perfect friend.* Someone who would agree with me most of the time, and other times we could have interesting debates and arguments.

Someone who would do the things I liked to do, or teach me how to do new things, and help me be brave enough to try them. Someone who would think I was funny all the time. Someone who would always be by my side, no matter what.

Just as I was sinking further into my bad mood, thinking that maybe the solution was to never leave my bedroom again, Mom stuck her head in the door. "Hey, kiddo," she said. "I forgot to mention, sorry. I saw Mr. MacMillan earlier, and he said that he has some work for you to do if you want to go over there today. He asked me yesterday, but I told him you had homework and had to wait until the end of the week. I still want you to do some homework before you go, so that it doesn't all get left for Sunday."

And with that, the clouds parted. I sat straight up. "I finished my homework! Well, most of it!" Since I had no one to hang out with at recess, and since the math assignments this week were review from last year, I had finished that quickly. We were also supposed to read the first chapter of *The Watsons Go to Birmingham*, but Auntie Lou had read that book with me over the summer, and I already knew the whole story. So I was mostly good. I hopped off the bed. "Homework is handled! Can I go now?"

Mom laughed. "Sure," she said. "You need to be home by six thirty for dinner. Tell him I said hello."

"Will do!"

I was already out the door.

CHAPTER 4:
KIND OF A MESS

MAC'S EVERYTHING STORE
IF WE AIN'T GOT IT, YOU DON'T NEED IT

The sign was painted in huge green letters, hanging above the doorway. This sign, and this store, had been here for longer than I'd been alive. Our apartment building was right next to the corner shop, which always seemed to be full of more stuff than could fit on the shelves, and it's the only place in the whole world I'm allowed to go without an adult to accompany me. I pulled the door open, and the heavy brass bells attached to the top clanged to announce my entry. Inside, it was chaos. But it was magical chaos.

Fruits and vegetables—fresh and nice, as good as

the ones they have at the big grocery store—were packed into wooden crates. Magazines, books, and school supplies were stacked in piles up to my shoulders. Nails, screws, hammers, and other types of hardware and tools I didn't recognize were hung neatly on a rack, next to a sign that said WE MAKE KEYS!!!! with four exclamation points. Mr. Mac could sell you a gallon of milk, fix your bicycle, put postage on your package and stick it in the mail, handle your electric bill, and give you gardening advice. He would sell you a bus pass at a discount. He sold yarn for the neighborhood knitters, toys and games for the kids, every kind of spice and baking ingredient for the chefs, tools for the construction workers, lottery scratch-off tickets for people who felt lucky, and he even bought a cappuccino machine second-hand and learned how to use it so he could sell fancy coffee in the mornings when people were on their way to work. Once, legend has it, Mr. Mac even got the paperwork he needed to perform a wedding in the store. It really was the *everything store*, and it was my favorite place to hang out. There was always something new to learn from Mr. Mac, and it was a good way for me to earn a few dollars, since he would sometimes pay me to sweep the floor or organize the shelves. Nothing major, but it was useful to have my own money for the book fair or to order from American Science and Surplus. Once, when his back was hurting, he even let me handle the register for an hour while he sat nearby in a folding chair and watched to make sure I was counting out the correct change to everybody.

Hearing the bells, Mr. Mac looked up from the

counter, where he was carefully unpacking gum from a box and arranging it for display.

"Miss Maya!" He threw his hands into the air. "What's new?"

"Mr. Mac!" Even though I'd had a terrible week, seeing Mr. Mac made me smile. I came up to the counter and, without asking, started helping him place the gum at the front. "First week of school. You know." I felt my smile disappear at the thought of school. I wasn't sure I wanted to explain myself, or that I would have words to describe how down I was.

He paused what he was doing, pushed his glasses to the tip of his nose, and looked at me dramatically. *"First. Week. Of School!"* He paused after each word, stretching it out. "My goodness gracious! And what grade are you in?"

"Fifth," I mumbled, without looking up from the gum.

"Fifth grade. Mmh, mmh, mmh. Miss Maya. You are growing up! Now, I know people change as they grow up. But I have known you your whole life. And I ain't never seen you talk about school without a smile on your face." He leaned over the counter, studying me carefully. "You didn't walk in here today with your first-week-of-school face on. Now, I think that face resembled your my-basketball-done-ran-out-of-air face. Or was it . . . your my-brother-got-the-last-cookie face? But surely!" He looked up at the ceiling and made a big show of running his hands over his beard and thinking hard. "Surely not your first-week-of-school face. What's that about?"

Man. The problem with being around people who know you is . . . they know you. Not so easy to hide your feelings.

"I don't know, Mr. Mac." I carefully slid each pack of gum into its position, making sure everything was in the right order and fitting snugly into place. Trident. Bubble Tape. Little blue and green and pink Chiclets, squeezed tightly into their plastic.

"It's been a rough week. My teacher is mean, and she already seems to dislike me. And my two best friends got put in a different class from me. So basically, I'm going to spend the whole entire fifth grade alone." As I spoke, I felt my face getting hot and my throat feeling tight. I swallowed and turned away, looking down at the floor.

"Aw, Miss Maya," said Mr. Mac. He opened one of the packages of gum and slid a piece to me across the counter. A sugarless one, which he knew is the only kind I'm allowed to have. "That sounds disappointing. But next week is another chance for things to be better. And you know what? You're a great kid, and I bet you're a great friend. Anyone would be lucky to call you their buddy. New friends will come. It might take some time. But they will."

I unwrapped the gum and popped it into my mouth, balling up the foil until it was so tiny I could squish it between my finger and thumb. "I guess so," I said. "What makes you so sure?"

Mr. Mac took off his glasses and distractedly began wiping them on the corner of his sleeve. "Oh, you know, the situation is familiar. This is what I always used to say to . . ."

He paused. It seemed as though he had momentarily forgotten I was there and was now remembering me for the first time.

"What you used to say to who, Mr. Mac?"

He looked away from me again, examining the glasses closely.

"Well, this is what I always used to say to Christopher." He tilted his head to one side. "My son. I guess I never told you about him, hm?"

I was so startled, I dropped the packet of Juicy Fruit I had been rearranging on the shelf. All this time I'd known him, and Mr. Mac had never mentioned that he had a son. Come to think of it, he didn't discuss himself much at all. I felt guilty for a moment, realizing that Mr. Mac was always worrying about someone else—me, his customers, the neighborhood. Who took the time to think about him? How come after knowing him my whole life, I never bothered to ask about his family? I leaned down to pick up the gum, and Mr. Mac kept talking, still peering down at the glasses and not me.

"My son, Christopher, boy, he was just like you when he was your age. *Just* like you! Always had his nose in a book. Always asking questions. Poking around, wondering how things work. If anything broke in the shop, he wouldn't let me hire somebody

43

before he tried to go to the library and see if he could find a reference book or some old dusty manual and figure out how to get it running again. Constantly sketching big ideas in his notebook, big plans.

"And sometimes, Maya, that boy's head was so full of big ideas that he had a hard time with the small stuff. Had a hard time making friends, or connecting with people. And you know what I would tell him?" Now he looked back up at me, tilting his head slightly to one side.

"What would you tell him?"

"I would tell him that when you have a big heart and a big mind and a big spirit, the right kind of people will see it. And if they don't see it, they ain't the right kind of people."

I stood in silence for a moment, letting his words hang in the air. Then I wondered something.

"Mr. Mac, where is Christopher? How come I've never met him?"

He frowned for a second, a frown so small and so quick that I almost thought I imagined it. It was gone before it was even really there, and Mr. Mac's face returned to its usually sunny cheer. "Oh, he went away to engineering school. Out there in California."

"California? So when—"

He looked at his watch. "Oh my goodness! I should get you started, or we won't get anything done before you need to head back home for dinnertime, and then your mama will be mad at me." Mr. Mac stepped around from behind the counter and clapped his hands together. "Ready to get to work?"

I straightened up. "Yes, sir!"

"Okay, that's good." He walked over to the storage closet. "Because I was wondering if you might be able to tackle this today. It's kind of a mess." He opened the door.

Kind of a mess. Talk about an understatement. It looked like a yard sale threw up in there. Boxes, papers, bins of nails and screws, an old stuffed Valentine's Day bear with one eye missing, a bunch of empty glass jars, an antique clock with a cuckoo hanging out, not one but *three* typewriters, a fishing rod, and several things I couldn't identify were crammed into the tiny storage closet. I had been complaining to Mr. Mac about the closet for months and bragging that I could get it under control if I had a couple of hours and some industrial-size garbage cans. A few things in there maybe could be saved and reorganized, but most of it needed to go to the donation bin or straight to the trash. There was no way I could get it completed right now, but I could at least start on it and come back to it another day.

Mr. Mac handed me a dust mask to keep me from sneezing, a pair of rubber gloves, and a big trash bag. He stepped back, stood up very straight, and saluted me, stiffly bringing his hand to his forehead. "Good luck, Captain Robinson!" He stepped back to the counter and set an alarm on his phone so neither of us would forget to get me home on time, and I proceeded to get to work.

I decided to start with something that seemed easy: a huge stack of boxes on the back shelf that I knew were full of old magazines. The community center had told Mr. Mac that they would take some of them for collages and other art projects, but I knew some of them were yellowed or had water damage. I figured I could flip quickly through the boxes and make a pile of the good ones and another pile of the ones that could go in the recycling.

Back in the store, Mr. Mac was playing Stevie Wonder hits, and I hummed and bopped my head along to the music as I was working. I was about to *handle* these magazines! They would be signed, sealed—*Oooh*. One box had a bunch of old copies of *National Geographic*! Including one from 1997 about the Mars rover! I paused to read it, then stopped. *Don't get distracted, Maya.* I set the magazine aside to take home and read later and kept humming. At the counter, Mr. Mac was showing off his classic dance moves to Terrance from down the block. Terrance came in the store a lot. I remembered when I was younger, and Terrance had graduated high school, and his grandma threw a big party and invited everyone on our street. Terrance looked so proud that day. His school had given him a medal for being on the debate club, and he wore it to the party. Through the whole party, he joked about it, walking up to anyone wearing a gold chain and waving it in their face. "My bling bigger than yours!"

Now he had come in to buy some milk for his two young twin sisters.

"What you know about this, young'un?" said Mr. Mac as he put the milk in a bag, doing a spin move on the tips of his toes.

"You got me, Mr. Mac! I don't got the moves like you! You'll have to teach me sometime." Terrance laughed. I heard his footsteps as he headed toward the door, then stopped and turned back.

"I almost forgot to get some bananas," he said. "We went through the last one this morning, and the girls will pitch a fit if they don't have some sliced banana with their breakfast tomorrow."

"Aw, shoot," said Mr. Mac. "The bananas I have just came in this morning, and they're green as can be. I don't want to sell you an unripe banana."

"It's okay, Mr. Mac," said Terrance. "I guess I'll catch the bus over to Super Mart and see what they got."

Hastily dropping an old magazine, I stuck my head out of the storage closet and waved my hands at Terrance.

"Faif! Ru don aff to to at!"

Terrance and Mr. Mac both looked at me oddly. "Er, what was that?" said Terrance.

Oops. I pulled the dust mask off my face so they could hear me clearly. "Sorry! I said, 'Wait! You don't have to do that!' You don't have to take the bus to Super Mart."

"You got a hidden stash of ripe bananas in that closet, Maya?" teased Mr. Mac.

"Nope," I said. "But do you have an apple at home? Or a pear? A tomato?"

"Oh, sure," said Terrance, looking confused. "My mother took her day care class to the apple-picking farm last week. We're drowning in apples."

"Got it," I said. I went over to the fruit stand, grabbed a bunch of green bananas, and handed them to Terrance. "When you get home, put these bananas in a bag, and put a couple of apples in there with them. The apples give off ethylene gas, which will help the bananas ripen faster. They'll be ready to eat by tomorrow morning, or your money back!"

Terrance looked impressed. Mr. Mac looked halfway proud of me, and halfway concerned about the "money back" part. "Don't worry," I said. "I use this trick at home! Guarantee you, it works. Or you can take it out of my pay, Mr. Mac." Then I popped back into the storage closet so I could return to work.

Terrance stuck his head in after me. "Thanks for the tip!" he said. "I appreciate—*achoo!* Man, is it dusty in here! Good luck getting it in shape." I waved goodbye, not wanting to take my dust mask off, and Terrance disappeared from the door.

Soon, I was back in my work groove, building a rhythm of stacking and folding and sorting and tossing to the beat of the music. Stevie Wonder's song about being superstitious always reminds me of my grandma. *She* is very superstitious. I sang along, and soon enough, the first box was empty! That was even quicker than I expected. I reached up and tossed it on the floor to be flattened later.

When I pulled the box off the shelf, it left an empty space. And through that empty space was . . . a face. Looking at me. I froze.

I screamed.

CHAPTER 5:
MEET RALPH

Mr. Mac came running in. "Maya! Are you okay?!" He had his fists up, ready to defeat any closet monsters that may have come after me.

I pointed at the face. "It's a—it's . . ." The face stared back at me silently, and I realized I didn't actually know what it was. Mr. Mac followed the direction of my finger, and when he saw what was looking at us, the worry melted off his face, and he burst out laughing.

"Oh, Maya! I admit it. When I asked you to clean the closet, I thought you might find him in here. But I sure didn't mean to scare you. And once you got going, I completely forgot about him." Now he was laughing so hard that tears were coming down his cheeks.

"About who?!" I didn't see anything funny about this.

Mr. Mac walked around to the back of the shelf, kicking empty boxes to the side. Behind the shelf was a tricycle and a scooter and a big trash bag labeled WINTER COATS. He moved those aside, and I followed in the path he made. Finally, we were staring right at the . . . thing.

Mr. Mac bowed low to the ground and swept his arm out to the side formally. "Miss Patricia Maya Robinson, please allow me the pleasure of introducing you to . . ." He cleared his throat dramatically. "Ralph."

I stared. I squinted. At first, it was hard for me to understand exactly what I was looking at. I had never seen anything like it.

The first thing I could make out was a large metal bucket turned upside down, with two enormous round shiny circles where eyes would be. This was the "face" I had seen—not a face at all. Or at least, not a human face. The shiny eye circles were rimmed with tiny lights, and beneath them was a thin LED panel that stretched across the front of the bucket to make a wide mouth. I gasped. This was the face of a—

"A robot," said Mr. Mac, as though he could read my mind. He laughed. It wasn't the kind of laugh you make when something is funny. It was the kind of laugh that comes out when you feel pure joy in your heart. "Ralph is a robot."

Was he ever.

I took a step back to get a better look. Beneath the metal bucket head that made him look kind of ridiculous, Ralph was sort of fancy. He had a barrel-shaped body. On the front of him was a panel with some gauges and buttons and meters of different colors. His metal arms hung at his sides, and when I peered at them closely, I could see that they had a million tiny hinges that would allow them to bend and stretch flexibly. At the end of each was a three-fingered hand. I held out my own index finger, middle finger, and thumb, slowly opening and closing them to imitate his three-fingered grip. Ralph's legs emerged from the bottom of his robot belly. I knelt down to get a closer look.

"Amazing," I murmured. Ralph had feet, sort of, but they were made of treads. The kind of treads you see on a tank—a rugged surface that could move across the ground even if it was bumpy or rough. It looked so familiar. . . .

I ran back to where I had been working, grabbed the *National Geographic* I had put aside, and flipped to a page with a close-up of one of the Mars rovers. You could see that the wheels were covered with thick, durable tire treads, allowing the rover to travel effortlessly across the surface of the Red Planet. I looked back at Ralph's feet. They were covered with treads. His legs were hinged at the ankles and knees, so it seemed he could go up or down a flight of stairs, but I imagined that the treads would allow him to move quickly across a flat or bumpy surface.

"This is genius," I said. "Really genius." I turned to Mr. Mac. "Who . . . Who made this?" He looked very seriously back at me and didn't answer right away. I stood up and walked around behind Ralph to see if he had some brand name stamped on him, a model number, some kind of label or something. I burst out laughing. The only thing on Ralph's back was his name, scrawled by hand in wide letters with permanent marker. RALPH. He really was a hodgepodge, this robot—a fancy high-tech body with a goofy metal bucket for a head. Feet that had clearly been designed by a brilliant mind, but with his name written in the same marker I would use to label any old school project. I looked back at Mr. Mac, awaiting an answer. He cleared his throat.

"Well . . . Ralph was built by . . . my son, Christopher. Do you remember I told you he went off to California to go to school? Well, the school he went to was Stanford University."

"I've heard of Stanford! They have some of the world's best scientists." I was trying to play it cool. When I said I had *heard* of Stanford, what I meant was I was kind of obsessed with the place. And MIT, and Georgia Tech. Any famous university with a big robotics lab. When I started getting into science, Auntie Lou had shown me some pictures of the laboratories and the things that went on there. It was a world of telescopes, lasers, incredible robots, experiments—basically, my dream world. Auntie Lou encouraged me by taking me to the library and getting me kits and books and videos on my birthday. In so many of them, Stanford was mentioned. Articles about scientists working on this or that extraordinary thing that seemed straight out of a sci-fi movie. If Christopher had gone to that university, he must really be about his business. "Did he build Ralph for a school project?"

"No, not exactly," said Mr. Mac. "Ralph was a hobby, you know? A fun personal challenge. Christopher worked at a robotics lab where he was always messing with fancy gadgets and doing complicated experiments. But he used to come home on school breaks, and he would help me out here in the store. He wanted to keep his mind sharp and give himself something challenging to do, so he started building Ralph on the side when business was slow. It was great for me, too, because I got to watch him, and I was able to see the incredible things my boy had been learning out there at that university. I was so proud."

I circled Ralph and looked again at his name. "Does RALPH stand for something? Like, um . . . Robotic . . . Assistance . . . um . . . Laser . . ."

Mr. Mac laughed. "Nope. Just Ralph. You see, Christopher was kind of lonely sometimes as a kid. He had a tough time making friends. So as an adult, he envisioned a robot that could be his buddy. A loyal friend." My stomach jumped when Mr. Mac said that. I could definitely relate.

"And when he was young, he had loved the book *The Mouse and the Motorcycle* by Beverly Cleary."

I nodded. "I know that book! I read it last year. And the mouse in the book is named Ralph!"

"Exactly."

"Wow." Ralph was really spectacular. Except for one small detail I couldn't figure out.

"Mr. Mac, how do you turn him on?"

Mr. Mac ran his finger over Ralph's name, letter by letter. "That, Maya my dear, is something I'm afraid I don't know. I don't even know if Christopher ever finished building him. I never actually saw Ralph in action. Christopher was always tinkering and poking around, adding new features, adjusting this, that, or the other. I'm not even completely sure he works."

Hm. I stood closer to Ralph and peered right into his shiny eyes. He was about six inches taller than me. I knocked on his chest and heard a hollow metal clang. "Hello? Anyone in there?"

When I knocked, his head shifted forward slightly, in a way that reminded me of someone falling asleep on a train. A tiny notebook slid down from where it must have been sitting on top of Ralph's head, and hit me on mine. "Ouch!" I picked it up from the floor and blew the dust from the cover.

"That's Christopher's notebook!" exclaimed Mr. Mac. "That's where he used to make his plans and drawings and notes about how Ralph was constructed." He reached out, and I handed him the notebook. He began flipping through the pages, shaking his head in astonishment. "This boy. My boy." He fell silent.

Suddenly, a piercing beep broke the silence. It was the phone alarm, letting us know that it was time for me to go home or I would be late for dinner and get in trouble. Mr. Mac looked up, startled by the noise, his daydreaming moment with the notebook suddenly broken. Then he looked at me very carefully. He was thinking.

"Maya," he said. "You are a brilliant girl. You always have been. And you have always loved science and technology. Would you . . . Would you be interested in taking Ralph home with you?"

You know what? I've never said yes to something so fast in my life.

CHAPTER 6:
THE BEST SCIENCE FAIR EVER

I managed to drag Ralph home with Mr. Mac's help. He loaded Ralph up onto the rolling dolly he uses to move boxes around in the store, and together we wheeled him out the door.

Outside, the sun was starting to go down. We paused for a second so that Mr. Mac could lock up the store and hang up a sign saying BACK IN 5 MINUTES! that I had made for him last year. I copied a picture out of *Alice in Wonderland*, of the white rabbit tapping his watch, and Mr. Mac liked it so much that he laminated it. As Mr. Mac looked for his keys, I took a moment to look around. The red and orange light from the setting sun made everything look prettier than usual. Across the street, Andre was stepping out the door in his crisp blue bus driver's uniform, getting ready to work the late shift. Usually, my mom says I'm not allowed to call adults by their first names, but whenever I said "Mr. Andre" he said, "You make me feel like a crumbly old man!" In my head, I liked to pretend that Andre was secretly a vampire, because he worked at night and stayed home during the day. When he was getting ready for work, he would blast house music so loud that if you didn't want to hear it, you'd better have some earplugs.

Sometimes he left his curtains open, and you could see him dancing as he prepared to leave for the evening. "See, that's the kick drum," he told me once at a summer block party as the steady beat filled the whole block. "That's what makes it *kick*!"

Next to Andre's apartment building, Miss Gina and her father, Mr. Armstead, were sitting on the front porch of their bungalow. Mr. Armstead was ninety-five years old and sometimes had a hard time hearing well or remembering details, but he always said hello to me when I passed by. Miss Gina worked part-time for a family that lived downtown, taking care of their baby and cleaning their house. After work, she always wheeled Mr. Armstead out onto the porch because she said it made him feel happy and calm to watch the street in the evening. Sometimes he would yell at kids if he didn't think they were doing something good, sometimes he'd read the newspaper, and sometimes he would sing a song he remembered from being in the church choir. "My father was president of the men's choir at First Baptist for twenty years," Miss Gina always said. "He may not remember much, but he remembers how to use them pipes!" She was the best cook in our neighborhood, and the smoky smell of rib tips or the sharp, earthy smell of collard greens was often drifting from her front door if you passed by on a Sunday or a holiday. For Christmas, she would sometimes make a caramel cake, golden and glossy, and would let me have a slice if I helped her clear the snow off her car and put salt on the sidewalk.

When Mr. Mac had finally locked the door, we carefully wheeled Ralph over the sidewalk, going really slowly so we wouldn't hit one of the big cracks or holes in the cement and accidentally send Ralph flying to his doom. I frowned to see some litter on the ground, especially since there was a trash can a few feet away at the bus stop. There's nothing I hate more than litter in my neighborhood, especially when someone leaves a glass bottle on the ground and it breaks—don't they worry that kids or pets might cut themselves?!

When we got to my building, our upstairs neighbor, Mr. Muhammad, was checking the mailbox. His daughter, Aisha, was behind him, absent-mindedly playing on her phone, and her big brother, Zaid, was doing the same. As we approached, the three of them looked up and did a double take, staring at me, Mr. Mac, and our strange passenger.

Aisha's eyes went wide. "Maya, what *is* that?" She adjusted her hijab nervously, and her text ringtones started going off right at the same time, as if her phone were jealous that she had stopped paying attention to it. Zaid chuckled.

"Aw, come on, Aisha!" he said. "You know Maya the Mad Scientist is always up to something. It's probably just her latest experiment. Hopefully it turns out better than your drone copter, Maya!"

I grimaced. Last year, I had tried to make my own drone out of some old remote-control toys I found at the thrift store, and it ended up crashing into the Muhammads' kitchen window.

"Don't listen to the boy, Maya," said Mr. Muhammad. "He has a lot to say for someone who tried to install a speaker system in his father's car without permission and almost set the engine on fire." He narrowed his eyes at Zaid, who blushed. Mr. Muhammad turned back to me, then looked at Ralph's metal bucket head. "Your project looks very . . ." He kept looking at Ralph, clearly trying to find something to say that wasn't too impolite. "*Unusual*. Have a nice evening. Tell your mother I said hello." The three of them collected their mail and went into the building.

"Yes, my mother, of course," I said a moment after they had gone.

"She'll love Ralph! Don't even worry," said Mr. Mac reassuringly. He lifted his finger to the doorbell to buzz up to our apartment—but the door flew open again. It was Mom, with Amir balanced on her hip.

"Hey there!" She smiled at Mr. Mac. "I was in the basement doing laundry and I heard you all . . ."

Her mouth fell open as her gaze drifted to Ralph. Amir's eyes went wide.

"What . . . is . . . that?"

I swallowed, and then I started talking. Fast, not

wanting to give any moment of pause where Mom could jump in and tell me no. "He's a robot his name is Ralph and Mr. Mac's son made him his son Christopher he went to standard um I mean Stanford you know the school in California it's famous anyway Mr. Mac said I can keep him and anyway how will I ever be a scientist if you never let me practice at home and he doesn't need food or water or to be walked outside and I'll take care of him I promise and can I keep him?" I stopped, gasping for breath after my nonstop babbling. "Please?"

She looked at me, then looked back at Ralph, then back at me. She seemed to be at a loss. Clearly she wanted to tell me no but couldn't think of any good reason to. What was she supposed to say? *No, young lady, no robots in the house?* She turned back to Mr. Mac for guidance. "Mr. Mac, how do you feel about this? And what does it do? Does it even work? Is it dangerous?"

He chuckled. "I'm sorry, Natasha. I should have called you first! No, it doesn't work. At least, I don't think it's finished." He hesitated, and in a flash, he and Mom exchanged a look that I didn't understand. "I gave Maya Christopher's notes. I thought maybe she could learn a thing or two. Might be a fun project for our young Madame Curie here. And if you get sick of having ol' Ralph in the house, you can always send him back to his granddaddy."

And that was that. Ralph was mine. My very own real-life robot.

On Monday, I sat in class, struggling to focus. "The blue whale is the largest mammal in the world," said

Ms. Rodríguez. "It weighs as much as three hundred thousand pounds. Is everyone writing this down, class? Good. The blue whale is made of Cap'n Crunch cereal. The blue whale loves bowling."

Okay, she didn't actually say that last part. I honestly can't tell you everything Ms. Rodríguez was saying about blue whales. Normally, science is my favorite, but on this day, I could barely pay attention. By the time we got Ralph into the apartment, it was late, and I hadn't gotten a chance over the weekend to really check him out or flip through Christopher's notebook. I practically bounced in my seat, I was so eager to get home and look it over. How did Ralph work? Could I get him to walk and talk? How did those special wheel-feet move? What kinds of things did the LED panel display?

Suddenly, the bell rang, and I snapped back to reality. Time for math. I reached into my book bag to find my math book, when Ms. Rodríguez cleared her throat loudly.

"Okay, everyone. Line up. It's time for us to go to the auditorium for the science fair information session."

The science fair. Today was the special meeting! At our school, fifth grade is the first year that you get to do the real science fair, the one with judges and prizes and presentations. I had been looking forward to this since I was six. Every year, my class would go visit the older kids and see their projects, and I would dream of the day when I could do something really special, something that would show everyone what a great scientist I was. And now it was finally going to happen!

We filed down the hallway, down the stairs, and into the auditorium. Ms. Montgomery was standing on the stage with a white lab coat and a table full of beakers. She looked unbelievably cool. And, I suddenly realized, if Ms. Montgomery was here, that meant her class was here! And that meant . . .

"Ay, Maya! Over here!" Jada and MJ were already seated, waving frantically. I waved back, my heart bursting. I missed seeing them during the day so much. Maybe I could squeeze in a few minutes to make some plans with them—they could come over and see Ralph and help me read through the notebook. Maybe not this week, not on short notice, but I bet we could make it work next week. MJ's uncle would pick up Jada and give them both a ride across town to my house. I would come out and say hi, and we would all hug, and we would work on Ralph together. We would get him to work, and then . . . I paused, realizing I was twenty steps ahead of myself. I probably wouldn't even get to sit with them. Nervous, I looked at the front of the line, where Ms. Rodríguez was sternly guiding my classmates one by one into their seats. When she got to me, the row was full.

"You can sit in the next row, Patricia." *There goes that name again*, I thought. But I wasn't going to complain, because sitting in the next row meant I got to sit with Ms. Montgomery's class! I nodded, spun around, and slid into the empty seat next to MJ. I quietly dapped him up and opened my mouth to tell him about Ralph, but he spoke first.

"Yes, have a seat, *Patricia*," he whispered. He giggled. "Why ain't you told her your correct name? Or do you go by Patricia now?"

"I don't know," I whispered back. "She's mean. I'm scared to talk to her."

"Hm," said MJ, fiddling with a fidget spinner in his lap. "I think you need to be RRB."

I was confused. "What's RRB?"

Jada leaned over and joined our conversation. "It means Really, Really Brave. It's something Ms. Montgomery says to us. Like if we're stuck or don't want to try something. 'You need to be RRB!'"

I didn't know what to say to that. I definitely wasn't feeling RRB this year. Or even RB. Not even kind of B. Mostly, I was feeling RRS. Really, Really Shy. I started to say so and to get to the business of inviting them over, but Jada kept talking. "Did y'all see what Juan Pablo was doing at lunch?"

"Ohhhh my gosh, yes," said MJ. "That was too much."

I felt myself getting smaller inside, and my heart was beating fast. Was I turning into an ant? What was wrong with me? I was almost afraid to ask, but I made myself do it anyway. "Who's Juan Pablo?"

"Oh . . ." Jada frowned, and I could tell she felt

bad. "He's a new kid in Ms. Montgomery's class. He's really funny. I'm sorry, Maya. I forgot you don't have lunch with us."

"No problem." I tried to say it normally, but it came out in a scratchy voice. I looked down at the floor, scared that I might start crying. My mind shot back to the moment when Ms. Rodríguez got my name wrong, and then to the moment when I cried on the playground. My ears felt hot, and I felt a lump in my throat, just as I had then. What was happening to me? These were my two closest friends, and now they had a whole other life without me. A whole language of secret code words, and funny stories about people I had never even met. Were MJ and Jada leaving me behind? I thought I might disappear into thin air. Just a kid at the end of the line, a kid with no friends, without even her real name.

MJ must have seen the look on my face, because he frowned, concerned. He poked me on the arm and quickly changed the subject. "Look what Ms. Montgomery is doing!" Up on stage, as Ms. Montgomery waited for the last few students to take their seats, she had quietly begun to do a science demonstration. She was pouring liquids from one beaker into another—and when she did, they would instantly change color, as if by magic. A liquid was a dark purple-blue in one beaker, and as she poured it into an empty beaker, it suddenly flashed bright pink. Then she poured some of the blue liquid into another beaker, and it instantly turned a vibrant green. Every time she did it, the students watching her in the front rows went *oooh* and *ahhh*.

"Now *that* is incredible," said Jada. "Isn't it?" She and MJ both looked at me, their eyes wide. I almost didn't have the heart to tell them, but Jada knows me too well. "Oh boy, here we go. Doctor Maya knows the secret behind the magic show."

"Sorry," I said awkwardly. "If you don't want me to tell you, I won't."

"No, tell us, Doc." MJ leaned forward and put his head on his hands.

I sighed. "The dark purple stuff is cabbage juice. It's an indicator, which means it can tell us if something is an acid or a base. The second beaker must have a bit of something acidic in the bottom, maybe vinegar or lemon juice. The other beaker has something that's a base. Probably baking soda. They look empty but they're not. We just can't see the small amounts from this distance. When she pours the indicator in, it touches the acid or the base and changes color."

"Let's give her a round of applause!" said MJ to an imaginary audience. Jada began clapping her hands in a tiny motion as though I had just sung an opera. "Bravo, bravo!"

I smiled. This was the old familiar feeling of being seen and noticed by my friends. They were always proud of my science knowledge, even when I insisted that it wasn't a big deal. Like in this case, it happened that I had seen the same demonstration at the Museum of Science and Industry last time Auntie Lou took me. The museum staff person even let me try it myself and told me how to make the cabbage juice indicator at home. Still, it was reassuring to feel normal again, even for a few minutes.

Just then, the auditorium got silent as Ms.

Montgomery began her presentation about the science fair. She passed out information packets with due dates, assignment requirements, grading rubrics, and lists of websites to use for research and ideas. But as she spoke, I could only think of one thing. I imagined myself on the stage, wearing a real lab coat, impressing everyone with my fantastic creation. I didn't know what it would be yet. But I knew I had to make this the best science fair ever.

CHAPTER 7:
HUSTLE

It was Pancake Dinner Day. When I got out of school, Daddy was waiting for me in front of the building, leaning against his parked truck. When he saw me, his eyes lit up and I ran to him, getting swept into a big bear hug instantly.

"My Maya! How are you, sweetie? How was school?"

"It was good, Daddy!" Which was kind of true, I guess. At least, it hadn't been a bad day. But how could I be in a bad mood when it was Pancake Dinner Day? I found myself smiling as I got into the back seat. As he started the car, I knew what he would say next. "Wanna go on an adventure?"

Once a week when he picked me up, Daddy

would take me on some kind of fun after-school activity, which he always called an "adventure" even though it could be something as simple as going to the library or to the playground. Sometimes it would be a bigger adventure. One time we drove far out beyond the city until we got to the woods, where we crept around, pretending we were spies until we spotted a deer hiding between the trees. Another time, Daddy had to get his car fixed, but we went to the same shop where MJ's dad, Mr. Randy, works. Mr. Randy showed me around the shop while we waited, explaining the things that were wrong with the different cars and what tools they would use to repair them. And once, Daddy drove me around the old neighborhood where he and Auntie Lou grew up. They had to move a lot when they were young. He drove me from block to block, pointing out which apartment was theirs on each one. Whatever we did, our adventures were always fun. And then afterward, we would go to the Cozy Corner Diner and eat pancakes for dinner.

Today we were going to the library. They were

doing a free workshop where you could learn how to use a 3-D printer, which I really wanted to try out.

"So," he said. "Your mother told me that you've been earning some money with Mr. Mac. That's good! Is he teaching you about how his business works?"

"Yep," I said. "He showed me how to do inventory, how to stock the shelves, and how to work the cash register. But sometimes I help him with the basics. Sweeping, wiping the windows."

"That's real good," said Daddy. "You know, Mr. Mac has been around forever. He's a hustle man."

"What's that?" I leaned against the window, watching the crossing guards with their bright yellow jackets guiding kids across the street as we sat at a red light.

"It means he always knows how to make something out of nothing," said Daddy, turning the car onto the expressway and passing me a piece of gum. He always kept two or three packs of it next to the driver's seat. "Back in the day, he started off with a van in an empty lot by the train tracks. He sold everything out of that van. In the morning, he had coffee and newspapers for people on their way to work. In the afternoon, he had snacks for the kids coming out of school. He sold gloves and hats when it was cold, and ice water and freeze pops when it was hot. He had pacifiers for the babies and shoe shines for the business folks. He *hustled*. He let the Girl Scouts put out a table to sell their cookies, and he also let the Mary Kay ladies set up there to sell makeup. Before you were born, I used to set up a barber chair there at the end of the summer and give everybody their back-to-school cuts. Soon he had enough money saved to move into the storefront where he is today."

"Wow," I said. I tried to imagine Daddy as a younger man, hanging outside with Mr. Mac in an empty lot, with the boys lined up for their fresh cuts and the whole neighborhood hanging out together, eating freeze pops and reading their newspapers.

"That's a good lesson to learn, Maya," Daddy went on. "Everyone in our family hustles. Me, your mom, your auntie, Poppy, Grandma, everybody. We work hard on what we love and figure out a way to feed ourselves off of it. And when things aren't easy, we learn to be flexible and cooperate to make it work."

This was turning into kind of a lecture—what did any of this have to do with Mr. Mac and sweeping the floor?—but I listened anyway, chewing my gum.

As if he could read my mind, Daddy said, "Anyway, what I'm tryna say is . . . I'm glad you're working with Mr. Mac. He can teach you a thing or two."

"I hear you, Daddy," I said. "I appreciate Mr. Mac. But actually, I wanted to ask you about something. When I was cleaning the closet, I found this really cool robot! Like, a real one! And Mr. Mac said I could have it! He said it was made by his son, Christopher."

When Daddy heard the name, I could see his hands tighten on the steering wheel. I almost didn't want to continue, but I did. "Mr. Mac knows I love science and technology. How come he never told me before that he had a real robot in the back of his store?"

Daddy was quiet for a moment. I'm not the most patient person in the world, but I knew that nothing I could say would rush him, and I had to wait until he was ready to speak. When he finally answered, it was with another question. "Mr. Mac gave you a robot? That's awesome! What does it do?"

"Daddy, why did you make that face?" His reaction reminded me of the way Mr. Mac got far away and spacey when he mentioned Christopher. "There's something you're not telling me."

He looked through the windshield, staring at the red traffic light rather than looking at me. "Maya, I'm gonna be honest with you. As a parent, sometimes there are tough conversations and I don't . . . I don't always feel ready to have them. And sometimes those tough conversations involve other people's business, and that makes it even more complicated." He finally turned and looked me in the eye, and I felt a tingle as he did. This felt like a very grown-up conversation. "You're getting older, and there are things when you were younger that we wanted to shield you from. And maybe that was the right decision, maybe it wasn't. I don't know. But as for right now, I believe some of what you want to know is Mr. Mac's business to tell you. It's not mine to share. Okay? Is that something you can accept and trust me on, at least for the time being?"

I nodded. You go your whole life thinking you want to be treated like you're older, but when it happens, it feels so heavy. "Okay, Daddy," I said. I didn't know what else to say. My head was swirling with questions and guesses.

Daddy reached over and pinched my cheek. He forced a smile. "So. This robot. What does it do?"

"Right now it doesn't do anything," I said. "It doesn't even turn on. But I have Christopher's old notes. I'm gonna go through them and see if I can figure it out."

"Well," said Daddy, pulling into a parking spot in front of the library, "if anyone can make that thing work, it's you. Just let me know if you need any help with it."

That evening, while Mom twisted her hair and watched the news, I read Amir a few of his little board books about the brown bear and the very hungry caterpillar and the pokey little puppy, until he fell asleep. Then I sat at the kitchen table with a glass of bubbly water and pored through the notebook.

It was the most amazing thing I had ever seen.

No matter how much we think we know someone, we can never read their mind. But reading Christopher's notebook brought me pretty close. It was a strange feeling, getting inside the head of someone I had never met. I didn't think Christopher would be angry that I was reading his private thoughts—after all, his father had given me the notebook, trusting me with it—but I still had the feeling that I was reading a diary. I felt a rushing, warm, buzzy feeling as I moved my finger over the neat lines of ink. And I was learning something on every page. Have you ever seen one of those behind-the-scenes things where they show you how a certain part of a movie or TV show was made? Sometimes they show how they did the special effects, or how the actors learned to do the fight scenes. That was the feeling I had when I read the notebook. I was peeking behind the curtain of something magical. Every page was full of notes, drawings, designs, sketches, questions. Christopher had tiny, clear, perfect handwriting, and he used different colored pens to write different things. Maybe he had a system where the colors represented different things? On some pages he had written BIG QUESTION in capital letters, and the question would always be red.

BIG QUESTION: HOW CAN WE DEVELOP A LIGHTER AND LESS EXPENSIVE ACTUATOR?

DAD BIRTHDAY SATURDAY!!! MAIL GIFT. CALL HOME AFTER LECTURE

BIG QUESTION: CAN BIOINSPIRATION MAKE ROBOTS MORE APPEALING TO WORKERS?

BIG QUESTION: WHAT IS THE BALANCE BETWEEN MAKING ROBOTS LOW-COST AND HIGH-UTILITY FOR THE HOUSEHOLD?

ACTUATOR TRIAL 6: FAILED ATTEMPT. TRY ALUMINUM ALLOY INSTEAD OF STAINLESS STEEL?

ACTUATOR TRIAL 7: FAILED ATTEMPT. ALUMINUM ALLOY LIGHTER, BUT NOT STRONG ENOUGH. TRY 6262 ALUMINUM ALLOY INSTEAD OF 6261? 6262 CONTAINS LEAD. HIGHER TENSILE STRENGTH.

There were a lot of words I didn't know, and at first I was pausing to look them all up. I found video explanations and definitions on the internet and wrote them down in my own notebook. It's a blue one I got for my birthday last year, with a really nice hard cover. I had been saving it for a special occasion, and now seemed to be the perfect time to use it.

Actuator: a motor that uses energy to move something.

Alloy: a metal made by mixing together different types of metal.

Bioinspiration: using nature to get ideas for building machines and new technologies.

Utility: how useful something is.

When I typed "bioinspiration" into the search bar online, I found dozens of interesting videos showing robots inspired by snakes, by ants, and even a robot that could jump like a kangaroo. "So cool," I said quietly to myself.

But after a while I decided to stop looking things up, and to let the words wash over me, skimming and taking it all in. I started looking for clues that could give me details about how to get Ralph up and running. It wasn't until about halfway through Christopher's notebook that I even got to anything about Ralph. I turned the page, and suddenly there he was, fully sketched out. It didn't look exactly the same, but it seemed to be the diagram Christopher had made to plan out how he would build the robot. A heading at the top said:

DOMESTIC/SOCIAL ASSISTANT. HOUSEHOLD? WORKPLACE?

*TALK TO DAD! HELP IN STORE?

In the margins were notes explaining Ralph's different parts. *Scrolling LED mouth. Camera eyes with remote viewing capabilities. Arms with modular actuators.* (Hey, I knew that word!) On the next page was a close-up drawing of Ralph's belly, with more detailed notes. On the page after that was his head. Each page seemed to be an instruction manual for how Ralph's different parts worked. After several of these close-up drawing pages, I got to one titled "Power Source." It had a list of options written in blue: *Thermoelectric. Long cord with AC adapter connected to power supply. Solar cells.* Each of these had been neatly crossed through with a single line. The last option on the list said *triple-Z battery.* Next to it were several plus signs, and it had been circled. I guess that's what he decided on. I turned the page.

The next page was blank except for one word: SUGAR. I guess Christopher stopped working on Ralph and started writing his grocery list. And after that, the other pages were completely blank. It looked like maybe he never even had a chance to turn Ralph on if he never got that battery.

My heart sank. In all of my library books, science projects were so simple. There would be a list of supplies and materials and clear steps marked *one, two, three*. When I followed the steps, I could make it work. I could make ice cream in a plastic bag, or a tornado in a plastic bottle, or I could make a circuit with an electricity-conducting potato. I knew that real-life science is about mistakes, about trying things over and over again. And there won't always be a library book to tell me just what to do. That much was clear from all of Christopher's "failed attempt" notes. But despite knowing all that, I still felt a pang of disappointment.

Maybe Ralph didn't even work.

I sat there, staring at the last page, then flipped through the notebook again. Christopher was so smart, so organized, so detailed. And he was a real inventor. A real scientist. I looked at the blank pages, squinting, as though if I wished hard enough, more writing would suddenly blossom onto the paper.

"Maya! Earth to Maya." I looked up. Mom was standing there with the phone in her hand. How long had she been trying to get my attention? I was so completely drawn into the notebook that I had forgotten about everything else. "Your auntie is on the phone. She got a museum pass from the library and wants to know if you want to go with her this weekend." I eagerly reached out and took the phone from her.

"Auntie Lou!"

Her voice came through from the other side, bright and energetic as ever. "Hey there, jelly bean! I was wondering if you—"

"The museum! Yes, I want to go." I didn't even know which museum. At that moment, I didn't care. I needed something to lift my spirits out of the disappointment I felt at the silent, lifeless robot sitting in my bedroom.

CHAPTER 8:
HIGH FIVE, MAYA

There are a lot of reasons Auntie Lou is the best. She always tells the best jokes, she always listens to me when I'm feeling down, and she always lets me pick a movie when I sleep over at her house. And when we spend time together, she makes me feel like the most important person in the world.

But today, I was hardly listening as we strolled through the Museum of Science and Industry. We had just finished walking through the giant airplane they have suspended from the ceiling, and Auntie Lou wanted to take Amir to see the baby chicks in their incubators. "How does that sound, Maya?" she asked. I think she expected me to argue, because I've seen the baby chicks so many times and I wanted to go back to the exhibit about tornadoes and lightning. But I was down for anything that would distract me from thinking about Ralph, so I just nodded. Amir rode along in his stroller, babbling happily as Auntie Lou pointed out different things to him. "Yellow, Amir! That wall is yellow! Oh, a train! Look at the train!"

Amir bounced in his seat and pointed at a doorway off to our left. "Go! Go! Go!" he said insistently. "Over there!"

Auntie Lou and I both looked toward where he was pointing. Above the doorway, a glowing neon sign said THE POWER OF POWER. My heart leaped. Auntie Lou pulled a museum map out of her pocket and peered at it.

"Huh," she said. "Must be a temporary exhibit. Let's go check it out! The chicks will still be there."

Inside the exhibit room were a series of glass cases and display tables with all kinds of power sources on them. I looked up at Auntie Lou. "Can I walk around if I stay in this room?" She nodded, transfixed by a glowing model of an electron.

I wandered from case to case. One of them displayed a replica of the "Baghdad battery," an ancient relic found in Iraq that is believed to be one of the world's oldest batteries. It was a pot with pieces of copper and iron inside, and scientists had done tests to show that the pot once contained some kind of acidic liquid. This reminded me of a science project from one of my books, where I made a battery out of a lemon. The acid that makes lemons taste sour could also conduct electricity. I turned to look for Auntie Lou so I could show her, but then I heard a voice from the center of the room. "Demonstration starting in one minute!" I hurried over to see.

At the demonstration table, a person with long purple braids and gold-rimmed glasses was smiling at a small crowd. They had on a lab coat decorated with colorful buttons and badges. One said "My other car is the Starship *Enterprise*," one said "Ask me about the periodic table!" and one said "Kai—they/ them."

"Hi, everybody!" they said cheerily. "My name is Kai, and I hope you're all enjoying the Power of Power exhibit today! In this demo, I'm going to show you a few different power sources and talk about how they work!" I squinted, trying to read the rest of Kai's buttons and badges. *Dream job*, I thought to myself.

"But first, let's have a quiz! Who can name all the batteries on this table? Yes, you! Wanna give it a try?"

Kai pointed at an eager-looking teen boy, who grinned confidently as he pointed at the array of batteries on the table. "Okay, um . . ." he said. "That one is double-A. And those are . . . C?"

"Ooh, close, but no banana!" Kai gave him a sticker anyway for participating, and even though he was old enough to be in high school, he stuck it proudly on his chest. "Anyone else care to take a shot?"

"Go for it, Maya," a voice whispered near me. I looked up, and Auntie Lou had appeared behind me. She put a hand on my shoulder in quiet encouragement. Amir was . . . a little more obvious.

"Maya!" he chanted in a rhythm, like my name was a song. "Maya! Maya! Maya!"

Kai looked over at our little trio and smiled. "Well, somebody has faith in you! Wanna give it a shot, young Padawan?" Kai winked as they said that last part, and pointed at my shirt. I looked down and remembered that I was wearing a shirt with Rey from Star Wars on it. I gulped. I don't like speaking in front of a lot of people, but . . . I looked over the line of batteries on the table. "Sure, why not," I said.

I stepped up to get a closer look and spoke slowly. "Well, like he said, this one is double-A." I looked at the next one, rectangular with two round terminals at the end. "This one is actually a 9-volt." Kai nodded. "This one is . . . This is a copy of the Baghdad battery! I just read about that over there, in the exhibit case. Um . . ."

I could feel everyone looking at me, curious and waiting, and my ears started getting hot. But I felt Auntie Lou's hand on my shoulder and tried to ignore everyone else. "This one is a lithium-ion battery. It's what they use in cell phones. This one is another really old type of battery that Benjamin Franklin used to experiment with. It's called a Leyden jar." Behind me, I could hear the teen boy whisper loudly, "How did she know that?"

My ears got hotter. "I saw it in a book about electronics." Auntie Lou turned and spoke directly to the boy, loudly.

"She saw it in a book!"

Kai nodded approvingly and smiled at me. "And how about the last one?"

"Well, that's not technically a battery," I said, looking at the shiny black thing at the end of the table. "It's part of a solar panel."

"Phennnnnomenal!" Kai shouted. "What's your name, kiddo?"

I took a deep breath, willing my ears to return to normal. "Maya."

"Let's give Maya a hand, everybody!" The crowd clapped approvingly. Auntie Lou tried to be slick about taking a picture of me on her phone in front of the table, but she was so obvious about it that I had to turn and smile for the shot.

Amir decided to celebrate in his own way. Just as Kai was about to continue talking about power sources, Amir pulled a bag of Goldfish crackers from some hidden corner of his stroller and threw it at the teen boy. "Have some! Want foldfish? I share."

"Ooookay, that's our cue to exit," said Auntie Lou. She started to turn the stroller around, apologizing to the boy over her shoulder, while I picked up Goldfish from all over the floor. I can get embarrassed about myself, but I don't get embarrassed over Amir. He's just a baby, and when you have a baby in your life, you have to accept that you're gonna find yourself cleaning up some "foldfish" now and then when you'd rather be doing something else.

"Oh, just a sec!" Kai called after us. "Come back in five minutes when the demo is done? I have a special prize for the Padawan here."

Auntie Lou nodded, and we hung around the edges of the exhibit for a few more minutes. She let Amir out of his stroller for a while, and I held his hand as he toddled around the room, looking up at the models explaining wind power and hydropower and geothermal power. He was giggling over a misty pipe that shot out steam like a geyser when Kai appeared next to us.

"Hey there!" Kai said as Auntie Lou wandered

over, still trying and failing to take candid pictures. Kai suddenly turned to Auntie Lou, startled, and squinted. "Wait. Ms. Robinson?"

Auntie Lou jumped, excited. "Kai Woodson! From Ogden Park summer camp? I haven't seen you since you were in fourth grade. Oh my goodness. Look at you, working at the science museum!"

Kai beamed. "Yes! Best counselor ever! It's so great to see you. I'm in college now. Been an intern here for three months." They turned to me. "And I have to tell you something. I've done that quiz a hundred times. And you're the first one to ever get all those power sources right." I gaped up at them, unsure what to say. Didn't other people read about the Baghdad battery? The glass case explaining what it was was right there in the room!

"So," Kai continued, "I have a special prize for you." They reached into their lab coat and pulled out a big red envelope with a flourish. "This is a gift certificate to the museum store! I hope you get yourself something special."

My jaw dropped. "Thank you!" That didn't feel

like enough, but I didn't know what else to say.

"You earned it!" said Kai. "See you around, Padawan."

I stood there for a few seconds, staring down at my red envelope. Then, suddenly, I ran after Kai. They turned around as I tugged slightly on the back of their lab coat.

"Um, sorry to bother you," I said. "But I have a question. Have you ever heard of something called a triple-Z battery?"

Kai paused, looking up at the ceiling before snapping their fingers. "Triple-Z . . . Why does that sound familiar? Oh, yes! I know!" They leaned toward Auntie Lou, speaking in a low voice. "Hey, I'm on break right now. We do have one of those batteries, and it's in the back. Since it's Counselor Lou and all . . . I can show you if you want. Just a quick peek."

I gave Auntie Lou my best puppy-dog face. "Please, please, please? Just a quick peek?"

Auntie Lou looked at her watch, then nodded. "Sure, just for a minute. Then we need to keep moving because Amir has to nap soon."

Kai led us through a door that said STAFF ONLY. I looked around, trying to catch a glimpse of all the secrets behind the exhibit. Lab tables covered in electrical components stood throughout the room, and museum staff with goggles on leaned over their work. "Hey, Kai!" said one as we passed. "Giving a little fan tour?"

"You know it!" said Kai, waving back. *Super-duper next level ultimate extreme dream job,* I thought. "Here it is," said Kai, gesturing toward a counter with . . . well, with a giant battery on it. I'm not sure what I expected.

Auntie Lou, frowning, apparently felt the same way. "Is there something that makes this battery special or different?"

Kai nodded eagerly. "Remember when Maya identified the lithium-ion battery on the table? Well, it's true that those are the batteries we use in our phones. They're small and cheap. But making them is bad for the environment, and they create a lot of waste. And the people who mine the metals to make the batteries have really tough working conditions and don't get paid enough money. So the triple-Z battery is an experimental model that doesn't require lithium. It was invented by some scientists out at Stanford. Instead of lithium, it uses maltodextrin, which is a type of—"

I slapped my hand on my forehead. "Sugar!"

Kai looked surprised. "That's right." They looked at Auntie Lou, who shrugged.

"She reads the whole side of the cereal box, this one," she explained.

It was true. One time when Amir was throwing a morning tantrum and I had nothing to do with myself, I spent twenty minutes looking up the ingredients in my morning cereal, just to see what all those things with the long names are. *Maltodextrin*. A type of sugar. *That's* why Christopher wrote "sugar" in his notebook. It wasn't a shopping list at all. It was an idea for a battery prototype.

Breaking out of the cloud of my own brain, I looked back up at Kai. "Do you know where I can get one of these?" I asked. "I need it for a project."

Kai paused for a moment, thinking carefully.

"How much do you love science, Padawan Maya?"

"A lot," I said truthfully. "A lot, a lot, a lot."

Kai ran their finger back and forth over their chin. "I can tell that that is true. Okay, well, listen. We had one of these batteries out for display, and then it malfunctioned. So we ordered a replacement. They're hard to get, because it's just a prototype. A model to show how an idea works. It's not something you can just buy in the store. The replacement came in the mail yesterday, but in the meantime, I managed to fix this one. So now we have two of them. And this exhibit closes in three days." Kai looked at me very, very seriously. "I can give you this one. If you don't mind the fact that it's, you know, used. And if you promise to use it for something awesome."

"I promise!" I squealed. All of the staff working at their tables looked over at me, startled. I lowered my voice. "I mean . . . I promise. Sorry. I'm just really excited."

Kai nodded very seriously. "Hey, I get it. Science will do that to you."

The next day after school, I made myself my

favorite sandwich: peanut butter and honey and banana and cinnamon and jelly. (The PBHBCJ may sound weird, but don't knock it 'til you've tried it.) Then I trudged into my room … and there, the battery was waiting. When I saw it, angels started singing and I heard the sound of harps and violins, and a mystical light shined down on it like the Sword in the Stone. Okay, that didn't *actually* happen, but it sure felt like it. I threw my book bag onto my bed and ran over to examine the battery. It seemed to stare back at me. *Okay, what you gonna do? Got something to say to me, girl?*

It was *huge*. Like the size of a small dog. Kai had wrapped it in plastic and cardboard for us, and Auntie Lou had hauled it up the stairs for me while I held Amir's hand. "You see," she grunted, her forehead sweating. "Oof. This is why your auntie goes to the gym."

I looked over at Ralph, who had stood in the corner of my room ever since the night I brought him home. Amir had thought it would be fun to play dress-up with him and had thrown a flowery hat on his head and wrapped a winter scarf around his neck. I went over and took the clothes off him so he could have some sense of dignity, but he still looked very funny. *What kind of expert scientist designs a robot with a bucket for a head?* I thought.

I dragged Ralph into the middle of the room, ripped the wrapping materials off the battery, and consulted the notebook. One page had a rear-view drawing of Ralph's torso, and there was a tiny square that was labeled POWER ACCESS. I looked at the back of Ralph's body. Sure enough, right where it was supposed to be, I saw a small sliding panel. It was so flat against the metal surface that I never would have even noticed it without the diagram. I pushed it, and with a quick springy motion, the back of Ralph's torso popped open.

Whoa. Inside, there was . . . a lot of stuff. I went over to my desk drawer, pulled out a flashlight, and shone it into Ralph's body so I could see better. Once I got a good look, it was definitely overwhelming, but at least I recognized some of what I saw. I got an electronics kit for Christmas last year, and the basic pieces seemed mostly the same. I saw wires, resistors,

LEDs, and . . . what was that last thing called? I went to my bookshelf and threw aside a bunch of old papers and Eyewitness books until I found it. *Electronics for Kids.* I had gotten this book used at a library sale, so it was covered in heavy plastic. I flipped through to the last page, where there was a photo glossary. *Resistors.* Those were the things that had tiny stripes and limit how much electricity can flow through a circuit. *LEDs*–those were tiny lights. I always remembered that because my flashlight said "high-powered LED" in bold type on the side. And *diodes.* That was the one I had forgotten. Diodes keep the electrical current flowing in one direction.

This was interesting, but I was looking for one thing: the battery terminals. Even though the triple-Z battery was enormous, I figured it should work the same as any other battery, with a positive and a negative side. And sure enough, right in the center of Ralph's torso was a large plastic casing. On the inside, the top was engraved with a small plus sign and the bottom was engraved with a small minus sign.

Here we go.

I lifted the giant battery and slid it into the battery case, making sure that the positive and negative sides matched with the plus and minus signs. I closed the back panel. Only then I did I realize I had been holding my breath. I exhaled with a big *whoosh* and walked around to face the front of Ralph.

His eyes were glowing.

"Ahhhhhhhhh! Ahhh! Ah! Aha! I did it!" I began to dance around the room. I had done it! I had activated a robot! "We did it, Christopher!" I heard myself say

it out loud before I really understood what I even meant by it. It was like, using the notebook, the two of us had cooperated to do something amazing.

As I danced, Ralph's eyes followed me with a tiny whirring noise, his motion-sensing cameras tracking my moves.

Suddenly, he spoke.

USER DETECTED. INITIATING INTRODUCTORY SEQUENCE. GREETINGS. I AM RALPH. ON SYSTEM RESET, NEW VOICE COMMAND REQUIRED. PLEASE STATE PRIMARY USER NAME FOR VOICE COMMAND.

I froze. Holy cow. This was the most incredible moment of my life. I couldn't believe it. I couldn't wait to—

ON SYSTEM RESET, NEW VOICE COMMAND REQUIRED. PLEASE STATE PRIMARY USER NAME.

My bad. "Maya," I said. "My name is Maya."

NEW VOICE COMMAND ACCEPTED. HELLO, MAYA. I AM RALPH. INITIATING INTRODUCTION SEQUENCE.

His head dipped down slightly, then sprang back up.

I AM RALPH. I RESPOND TO VOICE COMMANDS. CURRENT VOICE COMMAND KEYWORD IS "RALPH."

Right, got it. That was smart. Christopher had built Ralph to respond to commands only using his name as a keyword so he would know when someone was giving him directions or just talking. Similar to a phone, or a smart speaker. Without the voice command, Ralph would be overwhelmed by people talking around him and wouldn't know the difference between instructions and regular conversation. I wondered how well the voice commands worked.

Only one way to find out.

I got up and ran to the doorway. "Ralph, come over here," I said. He rolled toward me, his Mars rover feet going right over the blocks Amir had left on the floor, without an issue. *Amazing.* "Give me a high five." He stared at me blankly, silent.

"Okay. So you don't do anything without the voice command." Just as I'd suspected, talking with Ralph was a game of Simon Says—if you forgot the voice command, he wouldn't follow directions. "Um, Ralph, give me a high five."

HIGH FIVE, MAYA.

He held up his hand, which had only three fingers. So I guess it was a high three. Good enough. I reached out and touched it with my own hand. Okay, so he knew what a high five was. Had Christopher programmed that into his vocabulary or did he learn it from me? I needed to do some further testing. I looked around the room at the messy packaging from the battery. "Ralph, pick up the cardboard."

WHAT IS CARDBOARD?

I picked up one of the pieces and waved it in front of his camera eyes. "Ralph, this is cardboard."

CARDBOARD. SCANNING THE ENVIRONMENT FOR CARDBOARD.

His eyes whirred around, then he began to move around the room, picking up pieces of cardboard. "Aha!" I pounded on the wall in excitement. Ralph could learn! He could learn new things! After a minute, he stood in the middle of the room, holding a stack of cardboard in his three-fingered hand, patiently awaiting more directions.

I opened the bedroom door and walked out to

the kitchen, then called back into the room. "Ralph, come in here, please." He rolled out of my bedroom and onto the tile floor. I pointed to the recycling bin next to the back door. "Ralph, put the cardboard in here." He dropped the cardboard into the bin.

"Oh my gosh." This was gonna be a game-changer. "You . . . you can do my chores."

Ralph stared back, emotionless. His camera eyes were large and round. His mouth was a thin, dark line in the middle of his funny bucket head. "Ralph, can you smile?"

I CAN SMILE, MAYA.

Suddenly, a line of green LEDs appeared across his mouth, curving upward into a friendly smile.

I stared at Ralph. He stared back at me, smiling with that goofy green-light smile. This was easily the coolest thing I had ever done or seen. I wanted to show everyone! My mom, my dad, Auntie Lou, Mr. Mac.

And most of all, Jada and MJ.

When their names popped into my head, I suddenly felt sad. When would I get a chance to tell them? Or show them? And if I did, would they even care? Maybe Ms. Montgomery had a thousand robots that she let them play with every day.

I felt a wave of loneliness wash over me, and the lump-in-the-throat feeling came back. I reached out and tapped Ralph on his metal bucket forehead.

"Oh, Ralph. Maybe you can be my friend," I said without thinking.

Slowly, he reached out one creaky arm and gently extended a metal finger to tap me right back, in the center of my head.

MAYBE YOU CAN BE MY FRIEND.

CHAPTER 9:
A DREAM COME TRUE

In the corner of my room stood a small basketball
hoop. It was Amir-sized, short enough for him to
put a baby basketball through it, shorter than me. I
picked up the tiny ball and pretended to dribble it,
watching myself in the mirror, thinking of MJ and
Jada. "Boom! You don't know nothin' 'bout this! To
the hole!" I shot the basketball through the plastic
rim. "For two!"

Ralph watched me attentively, his eyes tracking
me as I moved across the room. I handed him the
ball. "Ralph, can you make a basket?" Ralph looked
down at the ball cradled between his three-fingered
hands, then back up at me.

MAKE A BASKET?

"Yeah! You know!" I pretended to fire off a jump shot. "A basket."

Ralph looked back at the ball. Carefully, he flattened it between his hands. I gasped. Before I could stop him, he stretched it, ripped out little pieces of the plastic, and shoved it into the shape of . . . I groaned as he handed it to me.

I MADE A BASKET.

I guess I had that one coming to me.

I've seen the movies, and the TV shows. Of course I know what usually happens when a kid brings home an alien or a talking dog or a monkey that knows karate or whatever. So even though Mom had seen Ralph standing motionless in the corner, a big shiny piece of furniture, I sort of expected that she would freak out when she came home and saw him actually talking, moving, and doing things. I was prepared.

When six p.m. came around and Mom came through the door holding Amir, an armful of mail, and last-minute groceries, Ralph was standing in the foyer beaming at her with his funny green smile. I stood behind him. I had put on a black turtleneck sweater, a clean pair of jeans, and fresh socks. I had even tried to do my hair. Never hurts to dress for success when you want to convince someone of something.

"Good evening, Mom," I said pleasantly. "Ralph, this is Mom and Amir. Tell them welcome home, and take the bags into the kitchen."

WELCOME HOME, MOM AND AMIR. I AM RALPH. PLEASE ALLOW ME TO TAKE YOUR BAGS INTO THE KITCHEN.

"I . . . I . . . I . . ." Mom stood there, her mouth hanging open. She let the mail drop to the floor. Ralph rumbled over and carefully took the grocery bags from her hands, then rolled into the kitchen, bumbling along on his tire-tread feet. Mom continued to stand there, first staring at the spot where he had been standing, then staring at me. Finally, she seemed to get her bearings enough to complete her sentence. "I . . . I can't believe you actually did it! Maya! This is something else!"

I smiled. Is there any better feeling in the world

than doing something that felt impossible? "Come in the kitchen and see." I picked up the mail she had dropped onto the floor and handed it back to her, then took her hand and led her into the kitchen.

Amir was already in there, chattering away with Ralph. Little kids are funny. He didn't seem to think there was anything unusual about having a five-foot-tall talking robot with a bucket for a head in your kitchen. He was on the floor, driving a toy car around Ralph's feet and making *vroom, vroom* noises. I thought Mom was going to get scared and grab him, but she was too busy being shocked again.

"Oh. My. Goodness. Maya. Who did this?"

The kitchen was completely spotless. Usually, when I come home from school, Mom's left me a list of chores, which I either rush through, half finish, or don't start at all. This time, everything was done, and more. The dishes were washed, dried, and sitting in the cabinets, not left out with a bunch of soaking pots. The floor was swept spotless, with none of Amir's dried Play-Doh bits or pieces of popcorn. The chairs were organized neatly around the table, and it was covered with a tablecloth and a small vase in the middle. On the counter, the vegetables we were going to have for dinner were chopped and laid out in small bowls. A perfectly made cup of peppermint tea sat next to them.

I beamed. "It was Ralph, Mom. He did everything, with my direction. He even can do some things I can't do. Like, he has stretchy arms, so he can reach the high shelf where the vase was."

She sat down in a chair and looked around, stunned. "This is phenomenal," she said. She looked at Ralph and spoke to him slowly, her voice raised. "YOU ARE VERY! HELPFUL!" He looked back at her silently. "Does he understand what I'm saying?"

"Yes," I said. "He seems to be able to learn new words and pick up on things I teach him. Like before you came, he organized some empty grocery bags, so I knew he would know what those are. But he doesn't generally speak or do anything unless you say his name. That's like his remote-control *on* switch. So, try saying his name first."

"Okay," Mom said slowly. "Ralph, you are very helpful!"

THANK YOU, MOM.

A panel of hearts slid across his LED mouth. Mom laughed.

"I taught him that!" I said.

"Well," said Mom, "Ralph is quite the charmer. And you are quite the scientist." Amir toddled over to her and grabbed her pants leg.

"Hungee! Hungee, Mama."

Mom picked him up. "Let me get dinner ready." She walked over to the trash can to throw away a piece of gum she had been chewing. "Oh, Maya. I'm so sorry to ask you to do another chore. But do you mind taking the garbage out?"

I beamed at her angelically. "Noooo problem." This was my perfect chance to try something I had wanted to do earlier, but to be safe I wanted to wait until Mom came home.

I wanted to see if Ralph could go up and down stairs. I had been staring at his big rover-tread feet the whole afternoon. They rolled easily over the flat ground, but was that it? In Christopher's drawings, I could see that Ralph had a complicated set of actuators in his legs.

These motors were small, but strong, and they were supposed to allow him to be able to bend his knees to climb up and down stairs and even jump. But did they really work? I was nervous. What if Ralph fell down the stairs and broke into a million pieces and I couldn't fix him? On the other hand, if he couldn't use the stairs he'd have to stay in the apartment forever. That wouldn't be very fun or useful.

I pulled the trash bag out of the can, twist-tied it shut, and handed it to Ralph. Then I led him out the back door to the wooden landing. We live on the second floor, so there were two flights of stairs. We stood at the edge of them, looking down. "Ralph, do you think you can go down those stairs? What do you think? You'll have to use your knees," I told him. I lifted my knees up and down, marching-band-style, and pointed to them. "Knees, see? You won't be able to roll, or you'll fall down."

Ralph's camera eyes hummed and whirred as he watched me carefully, focusing on my knees.

I THINK I CAN GO DOWN THOSE STAIRS, MAYA. I'LL HAVE TO USE MY KNEES.

I didn't want to make Ralph think I was laughing at him, but I couldn't help but chuckle a bit. He was repeating words that I said, and it was making him a better talker. *That's the way Amir learns, too,* I thought. I guess that's how everyone learns language, babies and robots alike. "Okay, Ralph," I said. "Carefully, very carefully, walk down the stairs. Carry the bag of trash with you. I'll follow behind you."

OKAY, MAYA. CAREFULLY, VERY CAREFULLY.

He hoisted the bag and proceeded to the edge of the stairs. Slowly, he lifted one leg and put his rover-tread foot down on the step. He followed with his second foot. Then he repeated this process. With every stair, he put two feet on it at a time, the way a toddler does. It was hilarious. But he was doing it! "Ralph, good job!" I called after him. "Keep going!"

Finally, slowly but surely, he made it to the bottom. I ran down the stairs in about five seconds and met him there, jumping up and down. "That was awesome! Ralph, you can do stairs! Now you can go anywhere! Good job, buddy."

He smiled his green smile.

I CAN DO STAIRS. NOW I CAN GO ANYWHERE.

He held out his three-fingered hand.

HIGH FIVE, MAYA.

I laughed. Looked like this robot was developing a personality. "High five! And I need to show you how to dap. Here, do this, Ralph." I extended my fist to him, and he copied me. I reached out and bumped his metal knuckles. "Okay. We're not in the clear yet. Let's go take the trash out." I led him to the back gate, opened it, and pointed to the trash cans in the alley. "Ralph, these are trash cans. Open this one, and put the bag in the can."

I WILL PUT THE BAG IN THE CAN, MAYA.

He did it perfectly on the first try, which was good because I had been pretty scared we would end up with garbage strewn across the alley, and spilling Amir's used diapers would be an act of war against the neighborhood. But Ralph didn't drop so much as a crumpled-up paper towel. Mission accomplished.

We returned to the kitchen, where Mom was waiting. She made Ralph wipe his tread feet on the doormat and his hands with a sanitizing wipe.

"Ralph, just because you're a robot, don't be bringing germs in my house."

While Mom made dinner, I went back to Christopher's notebook. Now that Ralph was up and running, I wanted to look again at some of the earlier pages to see what I could find. I squinted at the second page, noticing something I had missed the first time around. A name, written upside down in pencil.

Meet Dr. Yazzie—Mon 9/14 4:30 PM Gates Building (check office number???)

Huh. I flipped to another page. Here was a bullet-pointed list with the title "Robot Companion Goals." Christopher had scratched some things out here and rewritten them a few times, as though he wasn't quite sure what should go on this list.

ASSIST ELDERLY?

STORE TASKS—BOOKKEEPING, INVENTORY (GREET CUSTOMERS? DELIVERY?)

ASSISTANCE WITH SOCIAL SKILLS

CHILD CARE (ROBONANNY??)

Clearly, Christopher had lots of ideas for different ways that Ralph could help people. People in need—elders, children. I reread "assistance with social skills." Did "social skills" mean not crying in front of the principal, or speaking up in class? I sighed. *Sounds like something I could use.*

I didn't have time to think further about what I had read, because Mom turned to me. "Maya, one very last thing and then I promise you're off the hook for the night. I forgot to get soy sauce. Can you go over to Mac's and get some? You can take Ralph with you and show him what you've done!"

I thought Mr. Mac would react similarly to mom when he saw Ralph in action and do the whole oh-my-gosh-I'm-a-shocked-grown-up routine. Instead, when the two of us walked in—well, one of us walked, and one of us rolled—Mr. Mac simply smiled and put down the crossword puzzle he had been working on. "Well, will you looky here. My, my, my. You really did it, Maya." He walked out from behind the counter. "I knew you would."

He stuck out his hand. "Ralph, hello! I'm Mr. Mac."

Ralph curled his hand into a fist and reached out to dap him.

MR. MAC, HELLO. I'M RALPH.

Mr. Mac laughed and dapped him back. "All right now! Not bad!"

"Isn't he awesome, Mr. Mac? And he can help you do things, too! He can help out around the store! I'll show you. Tell me something you need to get done."

Mr. Mac stroked his gray goatee. "Let's see now. Well, I got a shipment of some canned tomatoes in, but I don't have room for them out front. It would be helpful if Ralph could stack them on the shelves." We went to the back storage room, and I showed Ralph the cans. "See, Ralph? Stack the cans on the shelf. Like this." I demonstrated with the first one, setting it on top of another can.

I WILL STACK THE CANS, MAYA.

He pulled a can out of the crate and placed it on the shelf, exactly as I had done.

"Okay, great!" Mr. Mac and I left him to finish, and I went back to the front of the store to get the soy sauce so I wouldn't forget. When I brought it up to the counter, Mr. Mac had his back turned. "Mr. Mac?

Can I pay for this soy sauce?" He turned around, and I could see that he had been crying a little. He took a tissue from near the register and wiped his eyes. "Mr. Mac! Are you okay? What's wrong?"

He smiled. "Oh, nothing's wrong, Maya. Seeing you with Ralph . . . well, it's a dream come true. I'm so proud of you. It's what Christopher . . ." He paused and took a breath. "Maya, I watched that boy for so many hours back there, puttering and tinkering away with this dang robot, special ordering these strange pieces and parts from who knows where, mumbling to himself and scribbling in that ol' notebook you got. You have made his dream a reality, Maya. You remind me of my boy, you know. Both smart as a whip. And good-hearted."

Now that I had been through the notebook and I knew more about how amazing Christopher was, this comparison really hit home. "Mr. Mac, thank you," I said. "I can't believe you would trust me with something so special. And Christopher . . . well, Christopher is a genius. He has really inspired me. I hope I get to meet him someday."

We were interrupted by a blood-curdling scream coming from outside.

"RAAAAAAHHHHHHHHHH! WHAT IS IT?!"

Mr. Mac ran outside, and I followed. No one was there. The screaming was coming from behind the store. We ran around the back.

There was Mrs. Crespo, who lived around the corner above the flower shop. She was walking her tiny dog, Cholula, who was dressed in a pink fluffy sweater even though it wasn't cold out. Cholula seemed perfectly calm, but Mrs. Crespo was not. She was yelling and pointing her cane at–

Ralph.

Who had left the store and come into the alley.

And stacked every single one of Mr. Mac's garbage cans into an enormous pile stretching as high as the neighbor's garage.

"Ralph!" I called out to him.

I STACKED THE CANS, MAYA.

He smiled.

"Maya, you are friends with this creature? What is it? This neighborhood. Gets worse every day. Come

on, Cholula." Mrs. Crespo walked off, shaking her head the way she did when she saw kids stepping on her flowers or riding their bikes too fast.

When I looked back at Mr. Mac, tears were streaming down his face again. But this time, it was because he was laughing harder than I had ever seen him laugh, grabbing his stomach, bending over in half, gasping for breath as Ralph and I stood there, looking awfully silly in front of a ten-foot mountain of trash cans.

CHAPTER 10:
THE INVISIBLE GIRL

After Ralph deconstructed his trash can tower and I explained to him the difference between trash cans and regular cans, we went back into the store and I paid for my soy sauce. I was almost out the door when I remembered something.

"Mr. Mac, quick question. Do you know of a Dr. Yazzie?"

His face brightened at the sound of the name. "That's the name of Christopher's robotics professor at Stanford," he said. "Very kind woman, and very smart. A really good mentor to him. I got to meet her once. Her first name was... Janice? Janelle? Something with a *J*." He shook his head. "Boy, she would be happy to know you got Ralph up and running. Real nice lady."

Another real robotics expert? Hm. "Thanks, Mr. Mac."

Ralph and I headed home, and he helped Mom finish making dinner while I searched for information on Dr. Yazzie. "J Yazzie robotics Stanford" did the trick: Her biography on the university website was long. It began:

"Dr. Jacqueline Yazzie (Diné) is a Professor of Robotics at Stanford University and the director of the Center for Innovation in Personal Robotics. She is a global expert in the field of robotics, especially methods for making robots interact with humans in everyday situations. Her areas of interest include machine learning, artificial intelligence, and user-centered design."

Then it went on with a list of the awards Dr. Yazzie had won and the universities she had attended and the robots she had designed and invented. At the bottom of the page was a photo of her shaking the president's hand and receiving some kind of medal, and next to that, a photo of her sitting inside an enormous robot suit, holding up a steel beam with one of her robot arms and smiling at the camera like this was a completely normal thing she did every day. Below that was her email address.

Cool, I thought. *Just send an email to the genius scientist lady with the giant robot suit. No big deal.*

I wrote a draft of a message introducing myself, saying I had heard of her from Mr. Mac, and explaining how I had gotten Ralph to operate. I attached a video of him in the kitchen helping Mom and some photos of Christopher's notebook pages. I had Mom read it before I sent it off so it would look sort of professional.

The next morning, no matter how much I begged her, Mom refused to let me take Ralph to school.

"But whyyyy?"

"Cut that whining out, Maya," said Mom, hustling around the kitchen. "The answer is no."

"I'm not whining!" Okay, I was whining.

Mom grabbed some cereal and poured it into a small container to eat on her way to work. "Let's see," she said, dramatically tilting her head to one side and tapping her chin. "I can think of about . . .

twenty thousand reasons. Give or take." She started ticking them off on her fingers. "He'll distract you. He'll distract the other kids. Someone might try to steal him. Someone might break him. Your teachers will be weirded out. And perhaps most importantly, you are supposed to be at school to do your *own* work. It's not fair to have a robot sidekick. Need I say more?" She looked at Ralph, who was helping Amir put his shoes on. "I mean, can you imagine him in gym class? He would *annihilate* everyone in dodgeball."

"*Exactly!*" I said, exasperated. "That's why I need him. To help me! And to be my friend."

Oops. That part slipped out. Mom squinted at me. "What do you mean, to be your friend? You have friends."

Yeah . . . about that . . . "Nothing. Never mind, Mom. You're right. He'll be here when I get home."

I didn't want Mom to know about how lonely I felt at school. Partly because I didn't want her to feel bad for me, partly because I was sort of embarrassed, and partly because I knew what she would tell me:

that I needed to adapt and make new friends at school. Which is a lot easier said than done.

Thanks to Ralph's help, Mom was able to get us ready for school a lot more quickly, and I got to the playground nice and early. But when I arrived at our usual fence spot, Jada and MJ were nowhere to be seen. I looked around, confused, until I spotted them standing off near the swings with two kids from their class whose names I didn't know. They were deep in conversation and didn't notice me. I thought about going over to them and saying hi. I even practiced out loud, whispering, my head down so no one would notice me talking to myself. *Hi. Hello. Hey! What's up? Good morning! Oh hi, MJ and Jada's new friends. I'm Maya.*

And then I thought about what their conversation would be like. Jokes and stories from Ms. Montgomery's class. I wouldn't have anything to add. Besides, what if the other two kids weren't friendly?

I went over to a bench near where some first graders were playing hopscotch and sat with my back turned to the swings. I pulled out a library book

from my book bag—one about the different layers of the Earth and the magma beneath the surface, with lots of pictures of volcanoes erupting. Off in the distance, I heard giggling. I looked up to see Zoe Winters and some of her friends leaning against the school building, looking right at me. Zoe was saying something and the others were laughing. I turned back to my book, curling my body into itself and tipping my face away from them. I turned page after page and pretended I didn't care about anyone. *Do not cry. Do not cry. Do not cry.* I looked down at a picture of a volcano. That's how I felt inside—hot as a volcano. Like a big ugly rock. Like if I wasn't careful, my feelings were going to bubble out in a red-hot mess, wrecking everything.

"I got that one last week."

"Huh?" Startled, I looked up. A boy was looking down at me. His light brown face was covered with freckles, and he wore plastic glasses that were slipping down his nose. He pushed them back up with his index finger. He was the tallest, burliest kid I had ever seen in the fifth grade. He looked like a football player.

"That library book. About volcanoes? I got it out from the library last week."

Without asking, he reached out and took the book from my hands. I was too stunned to say anything. The boy flipped through the book, past the title page, to the inside cover. There was a yellowish paper pocket with the lined card inside where we wrote down our names when we wanted to take a book from the classroom library. At the bottom was my name. He pointed just above it. "Elijah. That's me."

I hiccuped. "I know," I said. "You're in my class."

He nodded. "I'm right before you in the alphabet. Elijah Reynolds." He held the book back toward me with one hand and held out the other, waiting for me to shake it. "I'm new. Moved here this year from Indiana."

I shook the outstretched hand, pretending I didn't see Zoe and her friends watching from over Elijah's shoulder.

"So how come you're sitting here all by yourself?"

Who did this kid think he was? "How come *you're* by yourself?" Okay, not the best comeback, but direct.

Elijah's eyes fell, and I felt bad for what I had said. "Sorry," I said quickly. "I didn't know what you meant by the question."

"I didn't mean anything by it. Just curious. Because you seem so cool. So I thought . . ." He trailed off.

I thought it was weird that you were sitting here alone, a friendless wonder. "My best friends are in the other class this year."

Elijah nodded slowly, taking in what I had said. "Might be a good time to make a new friend."

I stood up. "Yeah. Easier said than done."

The bell rang. I started moving toward the door, dazed. Had Elijah seen me stewing before he came over? Could everyone tell how frustrated I was? Why did he want to talk to me, anyway? I stood up straight, trying my best to act normal and just stroll casually toward the door.

"Hey!" Elijah called after me. His voice echoed across the playground, and I watched a flock of birds take off from a nearby telephone wire as he shouted. I spun around, mortified, as everyone else on the playground turned to look at us.

Elijah jogged to catch up with me, then held out a hand again. In it was something small and blue. "You forgot your notebook."

That was the last conversation I had with anyone at school that day. After that, I pretty much went through the motions, not really talking to anyone, doing my work and keeping my head down to avoid trouble from Zoe or Ms. Rodríguez or anybody else. I pretended I was an invisible girl. During independent reading time, I read *Freaky Friday*, about a kid who switches bodies with her mom one day. I thought about how it would feel to change my identity and become someone else. Someone as popular as Zoe, or as brilliant as Christopher or Dr. Yazzie, or as helpful as Mr. Mac. Just to try on someone else's life for a day and not be Maya anymore.

CHAPTER 11:
RALPH HELPS

I don't know why I love Sunday morning grocery shopping so much. I love the sights and sounds of the store. I love the way people concentrate hard when they're looking at a piece of fruit and deciding whether to get it. I love the cereal aisle and the different colors and boxes. I love seeing people who come to the store straight from church, all dressed up, especially the older ladies with their big hats. Another thing is that my mom works a lot during the week, and I don't always get to spend as much time with her as I wish I did. So I appreciate the slowness of moving up and down the aisles together, in no hurry.

On this Sunday, Ralph got to join us for the first

time at the store, and he was winning a lot of points with Mom.

"Ralph, I need three pounds of sweet potatoes," Mom said. Over by the scale, there were a couple of people waiting to measure out the weight of their fruits and vegetables. But when you bring your own robot to the store, there's no need to wait for the scale. Ralph picked up some potatoes, holding them tightly in his arms. He paused for a moment, then delicately replaced one of the potatoes to the display and picked up a smaller one. Then, satisfied, he beamed at Mom and handed them to her.

HERE ARE THE SWEET POTATOES, MOM. THEY ARE NINETY CENTS PER POUND. I AM DEDUCTING TWO DOLLARS AND SEVENTY CENTS FROM OUR GROCERY BUDGET. REMAINING BUDGET IS FORTY DOLLARS AND EIGHT CENTS.

"Thank you, Ralph!" said Mom, tying the potatoes into a bag and putting them in the shopping cart. Amir, sitting in the child seat, kicked his legs happily.

"Swee-tatoes!" he sang out. Amir loved mashed sweet potatoes. You'd think they were candy, the way he attacked them when you put them in front of him. Ralph wiggled his fingers at him and pushed the cart along, following behind Mom as she headed toward the dairy section. She looked carefree and relaxed.

"It's so nice not to have to push that heavy cart!" she said over her shoulder. "Ralph, what's next on the list?"

ITEMS REQUIRED FROM THE DAIRY SECTION ARE YOGURT, TWO PERCENT MILK, AND STRING CHEESE.

"Got it," said Mom. She took a peek at her watch. "At this rate, we're going to get done so quickly, Maya. We'll have plenty of time today to work on your science fair project. Did you have any ideas about what you wanna do?"

"Mmm." I trotted along to catch up with Mom, walking beside her as Amir and Ralph trailed behind us. As we moved through the store, some people stopped and stared at our family, but Ralph didn't seem to notice. He was playing peek-a-boo with Amir, his lighted eyes flashing and blinking as Amir giggled and covered and uncovered his face.

"I was thinking . . . something related to feelings and the brain. Like, how we process our emotions."

Mom tilted her head to the side. "That sounds interesting," she said. "How did you come to that idea?"

When she asked that question, my mind leaped back to a moment from my school day on Friday. During quiet reading time, I had grabbed a book about Katherine Johnson and another book about Daniel Hale Williams and stacked them neatly on the corner of my desk, thinking I would use one of them for my next book report. In the meantime, I opened a book about Bessie Coleman and started reading the introduction. I read lots of different kinds of books, but lately I have been enjoying a lot of nonfiction and biographies.

I was totally sucked into Bessie's story. Just when she was about to travel to Paris to get her pilot's license, a shadow suddenly crossed my desk. I looked up to see Zoe there.

"Hi, Patricia," she hissed, making the soft *sh* sound in the name last for a few extra seconds. "I really wanted to read this book." She picked up the Katherine Johnson book from the top of my stack, smirked, and started to walk away.

I gasped. "But that's my—"

"Patricia! Zoe! Are you not aware that this is *quiet* reading time?" Ms. Rodríguez called out from the back of the room, where she was having a one-on-one meeting with someone.

"Sorry, Ms. Rodríguez," said Zoe. "Just sharpening my pencil." She brandished the pencil in the air and walked away toward the sharpener, my book tucked under her arm.

As I watched her go, my heart was beating really fast. I wanted to do something—to tell on her, to jump up and snatch my book back, to go to her desk and take one of *her* books. Something. But I had that weird feeling again of time slowing down. *Why are my feelings like this?* I wondered. *Why do I let Zoe have such an effect on me?*

Now, back in the grocery store, I struggled to answer Mom's question.

"I guess sometimes . . . I have . . . a lot of confusing

feelings," I said. "Especially in school. I feel sad, or lonely, or angry at somebody. And I wish I could control them."

Mom stopped what she was doing immediately and turned to face me. She leaned down and tilted my chin up so she could look right into my face.

"Oh, my girl." She sighed. "Everyone wishes that sometimes. Our feelings are part of what makes us human, but they also make being human so very complicated. And sometimes our feelings disagree with each other! You can be happy and sad and mad at the same time." I nodded. Mom kissed me on the cheek and turned back to the string cheese she had been looking at. "When you're at home, you can always talk to me about your feelings. But at school, do you ever share these feelings with MJ or Jada? Sometimes talking to our friends about things can make us feel better."

I wrinkled my face up. "I used to. But this year since we've been in different classes, it's hard to find the time. And I worry that they are having a whole life without me."

Mom nodded sympathetically. "That can happen

with friends, Maya. And that's normal. As you get older, you and MJ and Jada might have different experiences and grow into different interests. And that's okay. That is part of how we learn how to be who we are. What matters is that you care about each other."

Deep down, I knew Mom was right. But what she was talking about also felt really scary. Why did things have to change and be different? Why couldn't they stay the same forever?

Mom paused in front of the shelf full of imperfect foods, slightly bent boxes, and dented cans. She inspected it carefully before grabbing two cans of black beans and handing them to me. "Didn't you get some new kids in your class this year? Are any of them nice?"

I thought of Elijah and the gentle tone of voice he used when he handed me my book. The other day when I got up to get a tissue from the front of the room, I had noticed him drawing volcanoes in a notebook. They looked pretty good, too. Elijah was interesting, that much was certain. But if I tried to start a conversation with him, would he get my jokes? Would he have seen Star Wars? Would he think anything of the fact that I don't have my own room, or that our apartment is small? I looked up at Mom, wrinkling my nose.

"Yeah, there are some new kids," I said at last. "But starting from scratch just seems so . . . hard."

"That's part of life, Maya. And—oh my gosh. Amir! Amir Charles Robinson!" Mom was flipping out.

I turned to see Ralph and Amir and gasped.

"Raf! Swee-tatoes!" Amir was clapping his hands and laughing.

HERE IS A SWEET POTATO, AMIR.

Ralph obediently handed him a sweet potato. Which would have been fine if it clearly wasn't the thirtieth one he had given him. Amir was sitting in a small pile of sweet potatoes, his head poking out so that he looked like a little brown sweet potato himself.

Mom shook her head. "Amir! I can't turn my back on you for one second. Maya, your brother is turning out to be quite the smarty. He must get it from you."

I started laughing so hard that my stomach hurt

and I could barely talk. "Ralph," I wheezed, "put back the sweet potatoes except for three pounds. We only need three pounds, okay?"

"Ralph, while you're over there, get a head of lettuce," Mom added, picking bits of sweet potato strings out of Amir's hair.

OKAY!

Ralph whizzed away, his arms full. Amir looked very proud of himself.

"Raf help me!" he said. "Raf help Amir."

I went over to the produce area to supervise Ralph as he neatly returned the sweet potatoes. The way he put them back, they looked more nice and orderly than any of the other fruits and vegetables. A grocery manager in a black apron stood nearby, observing. "That's some friend you got there," he said, stroking his neatly trimmed beard. "He's real good at that. Might have to offer him a job!"

I smiled. "Thanks," I said. "He likes to be helpful."

The man's friendly expression suddenly turned into a frown. "But what's he doing? I hope you plan on buying that, young lady." I turned around.

Ralph had *taken off* his bucket head and was holding it in one hand. With the other hand, he was carefully balancing some bright green lettuce on top of his body.

MAYA, I PUT BACK THE SWEET POTATOES. AND I GOT A HEAD OF LETTUCE.

I groaned. I guess Mom's right. Each of us is learning to be who we are—even those of us who are robots.

CHAPTER 12:
GOOD NEIGHBORS

Leader. I chewed on the tip of my pen for a second and then wrote a sentence in my best handwriting. *The aliens took the scientist to their ship to meet their leader.*

Ancient. The explorer gained magical powers when she stepped through an ancient portal.

Mom leaned over my shoulder, reading what I had written. "These are your spelling words for the week? Your teacher is going to think you're trying to win an award in fiction writing."

I shrugged, moving my paper slightly so that the tomato sauce clinging to her wooden spoon wouldn't drip onto my homework. "I think it's worth it to make the sentences interesting."

Mom smiled. "Good strategy! It probably helps

you remember the words, too." Suddenly, her smile vanished as quickly as it had appeared. "Shoot," she said. "I'm out of oregano." She glanced out the window. The sky was orange and purple as the sun was starting to go down, but it wasn't dark yet. "Maya, can you and Ralph–"

I had already pushed my chair away from the table, eager for a chance to take a break from my homework. "Go to the store and get some so that our spaghetti sauce is delicious?" I did a quick salute, like I was accepting an important mission. "You got it." I looked over at Ralph, who was busy helping Amir build a tower of blocks in the corner. "Ralph, let's go to the store."

OKAY, MAYA.

Ralph headed toward the door. Amir looked betrayed and mad at me for stealing his assistant. "Raf block!" He waved a block at us menacingly. "Come!"

"Sorry, Amir," I said as I zipped up my coat. "Back in a second."

As we walked down the block, I warmed up right

away—I almost didn't need my coat at all. I loved the feeling of independence as Ralph and I made our way to the store, me skipping and Ralph rumbling along on his tire-tread feet. When we got inside, an older man was standing at the counter talking to Mr. Mac. They were both frowning, looking frustrated.

"Hey, Mr. Mac!" I said. "Ralph and I are here for some oregano."

"Oh, okay, Maya. You know where it is." Mr. Mac paused, glancing back at the older man. "Say, Maya, do you know any Spanish?"

"Poquito español," I said, looking carefully at the labels of each spice in the spice rack and searching for oregano. Cumin, curry, adobo, basil . . . "We don't start learning it at my school until sixth grade." I turned toward Mr. Mac and the man at the counter. The man had a city bus map spread across the counter and was pointing at it.

"Estoy buscando el autobús setenta," he said, gesturing at the map. "Setenta oeste." Mr. Mac looked helpless.

"I'm sorry, sir," he said. "No hablo." Mr. Mac turned

to me sadly. "I hate not being able to help him. Mrs. Crespo was in here a few minutes ago. She would have been able to help." He looked back at the man and shrugged hopelessly. The man, looking disappointed, nodded his head in polite thanks, folded his map, and left, the bells ringing behind him.

Mr. Mac shook his head as I put the oregano onto the counter. "I wish I'd studied some Spanish in school," he said.

"It's not too late!" I said cheerily, counting out the money to pay as Ralph hung back near the shelf, quietly and neatly reorganizing the spices I had messed up during my oregano search. "You can take a class!"

"No, I know," said Mr. Mac. "But it's not only Spanish. We have so many folks around here who speak Arabic, or Chinese. I feel bad when I'm not being as helpful to them as I should, or being as neighborly as I want to, because we have a language barrier." He handed me my oregano, sighing heavily. "Ah well. Careful getting home, Maya."

That night, when my homework was finished, I

had washed the dishes, and Mom was reading Amir a bedtime story, I sat curled on the couch scribbling in my blue notebook. I couldn't stop thinking about the man at the store—what if he really needed help with something important, or an emergency? And Mr. Mac had looked so sad at not being able to answer his question. I jotted down notes so quickly that my handwriting, which is usually neat, was hard to read. *One-on-one coaching?* That would take too long. *Online learning—headphones?* But . . . yes! I made one more note, circled it, then went to brush my teeth.

The next day, after I begged Mom to take me to the library, I stumbled through the door to our apartment with so many audio CDs that my arms were aching. The librarian had been surprised that I wanted them or that I even knew what they were. "Everyone uses those language learning apps these days," he lamented.

"I'm kind of old-school," I said, handing him my library card.

Back at home, I dug through a pile of old electronics

in a milk crate at the back of my closet—mostly stuff Mr. Mac had saved for me over the years, and a few yard sale finds—until I found what I needed. A disc drive and an SD memory card. I pried open the first plastic CD case and got to work.

Just as the sun was about to go down, Ralph and I once again rounded the corner to Mr. Mac's. Zaid was at the counter buying a newspaper for his grandmother and some hair gel for himself. He waved at us as we entered.

"Hey, Zaid," I said. "Can you help me test Ralph on something?"

Zaid drummed out a beat on the counter absent-mindedly, waiting for Mr. Mac to count out his change. "Sure," he said.

"Say something in Arabic. Anything."

Zaid raised an eyebrow. "Uh, okay. Shukran. It means—"

"Don't tell me!" I turned to Ralph. "Ralph, translate to English."

THANK YOU.

I frowned. "For what? Dang. I really thought this would work." But Zaid was smiling.

"That's what I said." He grinned. "*Shukran* means 'thank you' in Arabic. One of the few words I know, honestly. I really don't speak it too much except for the words my grandma yells at me when she wants me to turn the channel on the TV for her." He opened the door to leave. "You're doing big things with that robot, Maya. Keep it up. See you later, Mr. Mac. Thanks for the discount on the gel."

Mr. Mac waved after him. "Shukran!" He turned

to me and laughed. "Maya, did you teach Ralph to be a translator?"

"Yup!" I tapped proudly on Ralph's belly. "I took out every copy of Professor Pangloss's Deluxe Audio Language Courses from the library and transferred them to an old memory card. Ralph is now fluent in Spanish, Arabic, Mandarin Chinese, French, and just for fun, Latin. So next time someone comes in here needing help in another language, he's got your back!"

Mr. Mac put his elbow on the counter and leaned forward admiringly. "Not bad, Maya. Not bad at all. Carpe diem."

CHAPTER 13:
A SAD FEELING

The next time Daddy picked me up from school, he seemed lost in his own thoughts. As I was buckling myself in, he turned around and looked at me with a serious expression that I wasn't used to seeing on his face.

"Maya," he said. "Today we're going to do something sort of different. I'm going to take you to Mom's house to do your homework for a while. Then we're going to go to Mr. Mac's store."

No adventure? No Pancake Dinner?! And the store? That was weird. "Mr. Mac's? How come?"

Daddy's face became even more serious, and his eyes looked sad. He hesitated before speaking. "We're going to a special event that Mr. Mac is holding. If it's all right with you, I'll explain it to you later, okay?

When we get to your mom's house. And I'll take you to Pancake Dinner tomorrow."

Normally I would have argued, but Daddy looked so serious that I only nodded.

I had almost forgotten that Ralph would be waiting for us when we got back to the house. It was the first time Daddy had actually met Ralph, since usually he dropped me off and didn't come inside. When Daddy saw him, his face brightened. He walked in a circle around Ralph, examining him as though he were a new car. He whistled. "Maya, you have outdone yourself!"

I smiled. Showing off Ralph lifted me out of my grumpiness. "Ralph, this is Daddy. Say hello."

Ralph extended his metal fist.

HELLO. VERY NICE TO MEET YOU.

Daddy laughed and dapped him back. "Ralph, how are you? What did you do today while Maya was at school?"

I AM DOING WELL. TODAY I FOLDED THE LAUNDRY WHILE MAYA WAS AT SCHOOL.

He pointed at my open bedroom door, and inside we could see a pile of perfectly folded clothes, sorted by color. The clothes looked so nice that they could have been on display at the store. They were crisp and free of lint or wrinkles or anything.

"My goodness," said Daddy. "You're really something. Let's see what else you got. Ralph, what's the capital of France?"

THE CAPITAL OF FRANCE IS PARIS.

"What's eight times four?"

Ralph was silent. "Daddy, you have to say his name first," I explained. "Ralph, what's eight times four?"

EIGHT TIMES FOUR IS THIRTY-TWO, MAYA.

"Right on. Now, Ralph . . . most importantly, can you get me a glass of water?" Daddy pulled out a chair from the kitchen table, sat, and leaned back with his hands behind his head in an exaggerated relaxed pose.

HERE IS A GLASS OF WATER.

"Very good." Daddy looked at his watch. "Okay, Maya. You two hang out, and we're leaving here at five forty-five. And do your homework, please. Actually *do* it. That means don't ask Ralph for the answers."

"Yes, Daddy." Ralph and I went into my room, and I asked him to start putting the folded clothes in the drawer. I tried to start my homework, but I felt ... off. I searched my feelings, looking for the right word.

"Ralph," I said. "I'm lonely. Do you know what lonely is?"

I KNOW WHAT LONELY IS, MAYA. LONELY— ADJECTIVE. BEING WITHOUT COMPANY.

"Well, Ralph, that's part of it," I said. "But it's, like, the way you feel inside when you feel separated from the people you care about. It's a very sad feeling."

A SAD FEELING?

"Yes."

The LED panel that made up Ralph's mouth turned blue.

INITIATING SADNESS COMPANIONSHIP SEQUENCE.

Suddenly, soft music began to play out of Ralph's head! And he began to sing in the most ridiculous robot singing voice I had ever heard. Well, it was the *only* robot singing voice I had ever heard, but still.

THE SUN WILL COME OUT! TOMORROW! BET YOUR BOTTOM DOLLAR! THAT TOMORROW! THERE'LL BE SUN!

As he sang, Ralph rotated slowly on his rover treads and then kicked his legs out from side to side. He put his arms up over his head and waved them back and forth, and then he put one arm out in front of him and—

"Ralph," I said. "Is that . . . Are you dancing? Did you just nae-nae?" I fell over on the bed, laughing. "Oh my gosh. Did you do a robot nae-nae? Did that really happen? I'm embarrassed *for* you."

SADNESS COMPANIONSHIP SEQUENCE COMPLETED. ARE YOU SAD, MAYA?

I smiled. I was surprised at the answer. "No. I'm not, actually. I feel okay. I might feel sad again later, and that's okay, too. But right now, I do feel better."

SADNESS COMPANIONSHIP SEQUENCE SUCCESSFUL.

His mouth turned back to green, and he smiled his silly smile.

"Ralph, you know what?" I reached out and patted him on his robot back. "You're a pretty good friend."

THANK YOU, MAYA. YOU'RE A PRETTY GOOD FRIEND.

He patted me on my back, too. I shook my head, chuckling to myself. *Sadness companionship sequence.* That must have been something Christopher programmed. Was that something I could do, too? What if I . . .

I grabbed my notebook and started jotting down ideas.

Visitor welcome sequence? "Hi, my name is Ralph. How can I help you?"

Different languages? Say hello, then the person chooses a language to continue???

Child care sequence—read aloud? Patterns for block towers?

There were so many things I could think of programming Ralph to do. So many ways to be helpful. I opened his panel and looked over a few things, then I decided to try some new voice commands. Ralph stood by patiently as I tinkered for a few minutes.

Then, my eyes fell on my math textbook. Oops. As much as I wanted to just come up with new Ralph ideas, I still needed to pass fifth-grade math.

I worked on my math homework for a while. It was really tempting to have Ralph do it for me, but I knew that my dad would check it and I had to show my work. Plus, I figured, if Ralph did everything for me, how would I ever learn what I needed to know? How would I ever grow up to be a scientist and win awards like—

Oh my gosh, Dr. Yazzie. Had she written me back? I pulled up my email.

From: Jacqueline Yazzie
Subject: Re: Robot

She responded! Already?! I let out a squeal and Ralph looked over at me. "Ralph, it's an email! About you!"

AN EMAIL? ABOUT ME?

"Uh-huh." I began to read it.

Dear Ms. Robinson,

Thank you for your email. I was very excited to receive it. Christopher was one of my brightest and most beloved students, and therefore I am not surprised to see that Ralph is extremely impressive. Christopher told me a bit about Ralph, but it is wonderful to see how well he truly operates. You mention in your email that Ralph seems able to improve his vocabulary and knowledge base by interacting with others. This is called natural language processing. It's a field of artificial intelligence in which Christopher excelled.

I also want to point out something else special about Ralph—his feet. Most robots are only able to roll, which helps them get over rough surfaces, or use legs and feet, which helps them navigate elements in the human environment, such as stairs. From what I can see and what you have told me, Ralph can do both using his, as you call them, "Mars rover feet." This is truly remarkable and may mean that Ralph could win some prizes and awards for robotics design.

If it's okay with you, I would love to keep in touch. I can send you some information about experiments you can try with Ralph, ways to test and improve his capabilities. Also, if you are ever in California, I invite you to visit my *robotics laboratory. You are clearly a very talented young scientist.*

Sincerely,

J. Yazzie

A very talented young scientist. A very talented young scientist. A very—me? Me, Maya? The invisible girl? I wanted to hug my computer. I went over and hugged Ralph instead.

He hugged me right back. "Where'd you learn that? Ralph, I guess Christopher told you about hugs, huh?"

CHRISTOPHER TOLD ME ABOUT HUGS.

Christopher. Where was he? When would I get to meet him? Was he gone from Stanford? Dr. Yazzie had said that he *was* one of her best and brightest students. Did he graduate? Did he become a professor at another university or something? I needed to know. If I could have a cool young robot scientist from my own neighborhood as a mentor, I wasn't about to miss out. I had to at least ask. I started to get up and go to the kitchen. "Hey, Daddy?"

But he was already at the door. He had the same

sad, serious face as before. "Maya, honey. Did you finish your homework? It's time to head out." He looked at Ralph. "And you know what? Bring Ralph with you, please."

"But where are we going?"

Daddy leaned against the doorway and was quiet for a few moments. He looked at the floor. Finally, he came into the room and sat down on the bed.

"Maya," he said, breathing a heavy sigh. "There's something I need to tell you."

I felt a surge of worry. Was someone in our family sick? Was I in trouble? Did Daddy lose his job?

"It's something I should have told you before. I *wanted* to tell you. Your mother did, too. But we didn't know how, and we didn't want to . . . Mr. Mac didn't want us to tell you. He didn't want to talk about it. Didn't want you to ask about it. And we didn't know if you were old enough. . . ." I could see he was struggling.

"Old enough for what? Daddy, is Mr. Mac okay? Is he sick?"

"He's okay," Daddy said, and my heart slowed down

a little. "But Maya, today we're going to a memorial service for Mr. Mac's son, Christopher."

I frowned. "What's a memorial service?"

Daddy reached out and drew me in toward him, hugging me tightly. "A memorial service," he said, "is when you gather to remember someone who has passed away."

I jumped up from the bed. "What? So Christopher . . . Christopher . . ."

Christopher couldn't be gone. Christopher was like my friend. He taught me so much through his writing. He gave me the gift of Ralph. Mr. Mac always said we were so much alike. It felt so strange, because in that moment, my heart was aching so bad for someone I had never met in real life.

Daddy reached out his arms, and I crumpled against him, feeling his heart beating as I pressed my ear against his chest and cried.

"It hurts, Daddy," I said, my voice choked with tears.

"I know, Maya. I know."

CHAPTER 14:
CHRISTOPHER'S GIFT

We stood outside the store, everyone gathered in a semicircle around the entrance to Mr. Mac's. I felt sort of uncomfortable, not knowing what to do with myself. *A memorial* service? An hour ago I had been daydreaming about meeting Christopher. And now ... I reached out to hold Daddy's hand.

He squeezed my hand right back. "You doing okay?"

I nodded. I still felt the hard, cold aching inside, but I wanted to hold myself together for Mr. Mac. Daddy had explained that Mr. Mac requested me specially to attend the memorial. "He said it would mean a lot to him for you to be there," he'd said. "And Ralph, too."

"But ... what am I supposed to do? Or say?" I had only been to a funeral once before, when my great-grandma passed away, but I was only three years old then. How was I supposed to act?

"I think you being there is enough," Daddy had said solemnly. "Just be respectful and you'll be fine."

Ralph and I stood together, with Mom next to Ralph and Daddy next to me. Mom had come straight from work. As I looked around, I saw other people from the neighborhood: Mrs. Crespo, holding Cholula in her arms; Andre the bus driver, wearing his uniform. Miss Gina was rolling her father toward us in his wheelchair. Mr. Muhammad was there, and Zaid and Aisha. Aisha was holding a tiny bouquet of flowers. Lots of faces that I recognized, and lots that I did not. More people kept coming, and every time I saw a new person I wouldn't believe that they could fit on the jam-packed sidewalk, but somehow they would. Despite there being so many people, everyone was hushed, murmuring to each other quietly or standing in silence. Some people held candles or notes or teddy bears. Just when I thought no one else could fit into the tiny space, I felt a brush at my elbow. I looked up to see the man who had come into the store with the map. He nodded and smiled down at me.

I leaned over to Ralph. "Ralph," I said, my voice low. "Try that new visitor welcome sequence, would you? Number three."

INITIATING VISITOR WELCOME SEQUENCE THREE.

Ralph turned toward the man and held out a hand.

BIENVENIDO, SEÑOR. ME LLAMO RALPH. EL NOMBRE DE MI AMIGA ES MAYA. ¿CÓMO SE LLAMA USTED?

The man looked startled at first, then extended his hand to meet Ralph's and shook it. "Buenas tardes, Ralph," he said politely. "Me llamo Señor Eduardo. Mucho gusto. Soy un vecino nuevo."

Ralph turned back to me to translate, but he didn't have to. Señor Eduardo's kind smile spoke for itself. I shook his hand, and so did Daddy.

Finally, as the sun was hanging low and red in the sky, Terrance stepped out of the crowd. I remembered seeing Terrance on the day I found Ralph, buying his milk. And sometimes I would see him playing basketball in the summer at the playground. Sometimes Mom would try to pay him to help carry our groceries or put salt on the sidewalk in the winter. He always said no, insisting that he help her without payment. I'd seen Terrance lots of times. But now, as he moved to the center of the circle, Terrance looked like a different person. He seemed more important somehow, moving with a confidence I hadn't seen, his head up high as he surveyed the people around him. He was dressed in crisp jeans, a pair of flawless Air Force Ones, and an airbrushed T-shirt. On the shirt it said, "In Memory of Christopher" in bright purple and green letters, and there was a picture of a young man. He looked like Mr. Mac, but with a rounder face. He had large, bright eyes, and he wore short dreadlocks. He had on a heavy-rimmed pair of glasses and he was smiling, but in an awkward way, as though he wasn't expecting to have his photo taken and maybe felt shy about it.

As Terrance began to speak, Mom reached out and took my other hand. She squeezed it, and I squeezed back.

"Good evening," began Terrance. "Thank you all for coming out tonight. Today we are here to remember my fallen brother, my best friend, a neighbor, a son,

a beloved member of our community, Christopher Jeremiah MacMillan, Jr. On this day, ten years ago, Christopher was walking out of this store, his father's store that he worked in so faithfully. And he was shot and killed and taken from us. He was only twenty-three years old. He was in graduate school and had a bright future ahead of him. That future was stolen from him."

I inhaled slowly. I had heard gunshots before, sometimes late at night. My mom always told me when I heard them to count to ten slowly, to think of a happy memory, and to say a prayer for the safety of whoever might be in danger. I looked closely at Christopher's face on Terrance's T-shirt as he spoke. I wished I had a happy memory of Christopher.

Terrance paused for a moment and took a deep breath before continuing. "Every year in the United States, around twelve thousand people are killed by guns. That's thirty-three people a day. And every single one of them had someone who loved them the way we loved Christopher. Someone who misses them. Someone who cries for them." His voice began to shake. "Christopher was a scientist and the smartest person I ever met in my life." When he said this, people in the crowd began to nod, offering side comments. "It's true!" said one person behind me. "He sure was," said another.

"Christopher believed in using his skills to make a better world. And that's what we have to do. Each of us. In his memory." Terrance reached out to where Mr. Mac was standing at the front of the crowd. I hadn't recognized him, because he wore clothes I had never seen—a dark suit and a very formal dark felt hat. "I am now going to invite Mr. MacMillan, Christopher's father, to say a few words." He took Mr.

Mac's elbow and brought him to the center.

Mr. Mac stepped to the space in front of the door of the shop. He took a deep, heavy breath and slowly removed his hat, holding it in front of his heart. As he spoke, Terrance stood next to him. He reminded me of a bodyguard, like Mr. Mac was the king of the neighborhood and Terrance would do anything to protect him and keep him safe.

Mr. Mac stood there in silence for a while. He scanned the crowd, pausing his gaze at various people who he recognized and giving them a small nod. Finally, his eyes landed on me and my family, and he smiled. Then he began to speak.

"Good evening," he said. "I am so grateful that you all came here tonight to help me lift up the memory of my son, my only child, Christopher. I tried to prepare a speech, but it was too much for me. So I'm going to speak from my heart.

"For the last ten years, not a day has gone by where I didn't miss my boy. He left a hole in my life as big as the whole world.

"And for a long time, I didn't want anyone to

mention Christopher to me. I didn't want to talk about what happened. I didn't want to talk about him because hearing his name, thinking about him, made me feel like . . . I couldn't go on. It made me feel hopeless. So I tried to go from day to day, not facing the truth about how I felt.

"Recently, that changed. You see, y'all, Christopher was a scientist, as Terrance mentioned. And he was a genius. I mean, *smart.* Even when he was a little bitty baby. And sometimes as a young boy, he struggled with that. Sometimes he felt lonely. Sometimes he had a hard time making friends, and speaking up for himself. And sometimes he wanted to try to be someone else. Someone different. But after a while, Christopher realized that he could never be anyone but himself. Oh, believe me, he tried! He tried to blend in. But he didn't have it in him, that boy. He was too special. And so he realized that he had to be the way God made him. And furthermore, he realized that he had something to teach the world. He could use his gifts to try to build inventions that would help people.

"As many of you know, Christopher designed and built robots as part of his university studies. But he didn't want to design robots to fight wars or work in factories. He made robots that could be friends to people in need. Robots that could comfort people in the hospital, robots that could help the elderly around the house, robots that could be a companion to a lonely child. He wanted to use his gifts to heal the world, to use technology to make the world a kinder place."

Mr. Mac stopped speaking for a moment. A tear fell down his cheek. Terrance put an arm around him, and Miss Gina stepped out of the crowd to hand him a tissue. When he began again, Mr. Mac looked right at me.

"Recently, I realized that Christopher's spirit is still with us. And if he were here, he would not want me to be quiet and silent and pretend nothing happened. He would want me to use his memory to teach, to inspire others. He would want his brilliance to shine on. And if only—if only he could see—" He cried, but he kept going. "If only he could see how his dream is still alive, he would be . . . he would be so happy. Just to see it live on.

"So I'm not gonna be silent anymore. I'm going to tell the world. I had a son named Christopher. I loved him. He was a shining light. And as long as a young person is true to their own spirit, as long as they use their gifts to help others, his light will shine on. His light will shine on."

Mr. Mac stepped away. Terrance invited everyone to the front, and one by one, our neighbors placed their candles and their cards and their letters in front of the store. I hung back, crying. I looked around, wondering if Christopher might somehow appear and tell everyone that it was a trick, that he wasn't really gone. I looked up at Mom, and she hugged me tightly. "Always remember, Maya," she whispered in my ear, "being yourself is a gift to others around you. It's a gift to the people who love you. And it's a way to remember the people who came before you, who made you what you are."

When she let me go, Mr. Mac was there. Both of us looked at each other, crying, and suddenly I felt very grown-up. Like for a second, instead of being a kid and an adult, we were two people who were sharing our

tears with each other. I didn't know what to say, but he spoke first.

"Thank you, Maya. Thank you for bringing my son back to me." He looked at Ralph. Ralph's eyes were whizzing and whirring as he looked around at the group of people leaning in close to one another and wiping tears away. He seemed to understand everyone's sadness, and his mouth had become a series of blue, downward-turned lights. Mr. Mac waved at him, grabbing his attention. "Ralph . . ." said Mr. Mac. "Thank you."

Ralph looked at me. Then he extended his arms outward toward Mr. Mac.

THANK YOU. CHRISTOPHER TOLD ME ABOUT HUGS.

The two of them embraced as the sun went down.

CHAPTER 15:
PRACTICE MAKES PERFECT

I was working in a lab. A state-of-the-art laboratory, surrounded by my projects: a six-legged robot, a robot that wiggles around like a snake, a tiny robot that can climb into someone's body and locate the cancer cells making them sick. My assistants were running around, taking measurements and observations on clipboards, typing away at computers, leaning over tables covered in electronic components and wiring circuits. One of them dashed over to me. "Dr. Robinson," she said, looking at her watch. "You have a meeting with the president in a few minutes. We need to head out." I nodded and told her—

"MAAAAYAAAAAAAA! I HAVE TOLD YOU! THREE! TIMES! Stop hitting that snooze button and get up.

You don't want to be late on Science Fair Day."

Science Fair Day. Science Fair Day! It was finally here! I jumped out of bed. "Ralph, good morning! Can you put my homework and books into my book bag, please?"

GOOD MORNING, MAYA. YES, I CAN PUT ALL OF YOUR HOMEWORK AND BOOKS INTO YOUR BOOK BAG. WOULD YOU ALSO LIKE ME TO GATHER YOUR SCIENCE FAIR MATERIALS?

"Yes, please! Thanks, Ralph. I'm gonna go brush my teeth." That was the other very, very special thing about today. Mom had agreed to let Ralph come to school with me for the first time. I convinced her using two logical points: One, my science fair project was too heavy for me to carry around by myself. I had built a model volcano connected to a heart rate monitor, and I planned to ask people a series of hard math questions. If the person wearing the monitor got stressed out or scared, the volcano would spill over. That part was a little bit of a gimmick, I admit. My hypothesis was that as the math questions increased in difficulty, people's hearts would beat faster. I had made the lava out of oatmeal and red food coloring, and I called the project "Don't Let Your Feelings Erupt." Not a bad twist on the old science fair volcano, huh?

And the second point I made to Mom was that it was Science Fair Day. So lots of kids would be bringing weird stuff to school. Ralph was less likely to cause a commotion or distract anyone amidst the mice in cages, Mentos in Pepsi bottles, and potato cannons.

I was glad that Ralph would be an extra set of hands to help me carry everything and set it up. Some kids' parents came to school to help them do that, but my parents had to work. Secretly, though, I was mostly glad to have Ralph there as moral support. I was nervous about the day, and I liked knowing that my robot friend would have my back.

At school, the cafeteria was bustling with activity. The lunch tables were set up in rows. Every single fifth, sixth, seventh, and eighth grader in the whole school was there, pulling enormous poster boards out of trash bags and balancing their materials carefully on tables. One kid had an entire fish tank full of fish. Another had a scale model of the Sears Tower built out of toothpicks. I was nervous just watching them.

I blinked and shook my head. *Get your head in the game, Maya.* I needed to stop being so distracted by everyone else's project and focus on my own. But when I turned back to the table, Ralph was almost finished setting everything up. "Oh wow, Ralph. Thanks, buddy," I said.

NO PROBLEM, BUDDY. HIGH FIVE. ALSO, I HAVE A VOICE NOTE FOR YOU FROM DADDY.

Ralph made a small clicking sound, and then a recording of my father's voice began to play. "Hey, Maya. I just wanted to let you know that even though your mom and I can't make it to your science fair, we are *so* proud of you. We know it will go great." And then another small click as the recording ended.

I beamed at Ralph. "That was so nice!" Then I felt another pang of worry. "Ralph, what time is it?"

IT IS CURRENTLY EIGHT FIFTY-TWO A.M.

"Argh. Eight more minutes until we start? I'm so

nervous! What am I supposed to do with myself? Ralph, what should I do?" I paced back and forth in front of the table.

YOU COULD PRACTICE YOUR PRESENTATION. MOM SAID—

Ralph clicked quietly, and a recording of my mother's voice began to play. "Practice makes perfect! You want to practice your presentation so that it goes smoothly for the judges." There was a second small click.

"Okay. Good point, good point. Practice. Practice. Okay." I stopped pacing, spun around to face Ralph, and—Zoe? Zoe Winters was standing there, examining Ralph carefully from top to bottom.

"Um. Hi, Zoe."

"Hello, Maya." That was weird. No "Patricia" this time. She was smiling her creepy great white shark smile. I mean, I guess it was a normal smile, but coming from her it creeped me out. Zoe was never nice to me. What was the deal? "Is this your robot?"

No, he's a random robot that showed up at school and is standing here talking to me for no reason. Never seen him before in my life. "Yep."

"Very cool. Cool project. You're always so good at science. I should have known you would have a good science fair project."

"Th—" My voice came out in a weird squeak. Ralph was not my project, but this was the longest Zoe had ever gone without being mean to me. Why correct her? I cleared my throat. "Thank you. What's your project?"

"Oh, it's over there." She gestured vaguely toward the front of the cafeteria. "It's a coding thing I did with my older sister. We made a memory game."

What?! That actually sounded really cool. "Really? That's awesome. Maybe if we get a break in the presentations I can go over and check it out."

"Sure, I hope you do. Hey, listen, a minute ago I heard you say you were feeling nervous. You know what always helps me? Getting a drink of water. Why don't you go get some water and take a deep breath, and I'll stand here and watch your project? You still have a couple minutes."

That was actually a good idea. I looked at Ralph, uncertain. "Ralph, will you be okay if I go get some water? I'll come right back."

I WILL BE OKAY IF YOU GO GET SOME WATER. YOU'LL COME RIGHT BACK. I WILL TAKE CARE OF THE VOLCANO.

Zoe's eyes widened. "Wow! Your robot is a good talker. Go on, we'll wait here for you."

I was torn. I didn't really want to leave Ralph, but Zoe was being so weirdly nice to me. If I went along with it, maybe the niceness would continue and she wouldn't be such a jerk to me after today. And she had a good point about the water. *It will only be a minute.*

"Okay, thanks so much! I'll be right back." I skittered off to the far corner of the cafeteria, where there was a water fountain. I tried to keep an eye on Ralph the whole way, but I worried that if I kept peeking back over my shoulder at Zoe it would look weird. And in order to drink, I had to keep my eyes on the fountain or else I'd spill water on myself, which was the last thing I wanted. Plus, the other displays were blocking my view. I couldn't see anything except tables and poster boards and . . .

MJ and Jada stood together, talking and laughing in front of a board. It must have been MJ's, because it had a bunch of pictures of his cat, Diamond, and the title said "Do Cats Recognize Faces?" *This was my chance.* I could go over, say hi, bring them to my table, show them Ralph. There was no one else with them, no cool kids that I didn't know. Just my two friends. They had paused in their conversation and were standing quietly. Perfect timing. I started to walk toward them.

And then the bell rang. Yikes. Principal Merri-weather stood atop a stool and shouted, "Welcome to this year's science fair! It is nine o'clock. Judging will now officially begin. Presenters, please head to your stations."

Shoot. MJ dapped Jada and she walked away, off toward wherever her project was. I hurried back to my table, already feeling thirsty again. "Glad you made it back," Zoe said. "I don't want to miss the judges."

"Yeah, thanks. Sorry," I replied.

"Good luck!" she said, smiling that weird smile again. And before I could say anything back, she skipped away.

I looked at the volcano, suspicious that Zoe had broken something. It seemed totally fine, everything in place. My poster board stood perfectly in the center of the table, the same way Ralph had set it up. And Ralph looked fine, too. "Ralph, you doing okay?"

I AM DOING OKAY.

Maybe I had been unfair to Zoe. I didn't have time to think about it much, though, because two of the volunteer judges arrived. One judge had a friendly, encouraging smile on her face and an enormous purse over her shoulder, the kind my grandma carries that always has twenty thousand things in it. The other judge had a necktie on, with a pattern of little atoms on it. *My kind of crowd,* I thought. I sprang into presentation mode.

"Good morning! Welcome to the science fair. My name is Maya Robinson and this project is called—"

"AAAAWWWWWW YEAAAAHHHH! WHO IS READY TO ROCK?"

What in the world? I looked to my left. At the table next to mine, an eighth grader named Marcus had a microphone set up, and his friend had an electric guitar. Their poster board said "The Science of Sound Waves: Investigating Rock Music." The electric guitar was plugged into an amp, and the noise was piercing. I tried to speak up.

"SORRY. CAN I START OVER? MY NAME IS MAYA ROBINSON AND—"

The judge with the enormous purse leaned closer to me, cupping her hand over her ear. "WHAT? SWEETIE, I CAN'T HEAR YOU OVER THAT GUITAR."

I gulped and tried to raise my voice even louder.

"I KNOW, SORRY. MY NAME IS—" The music

paused as the guitar kid started talking to the judges about his project. My nerves were shattered, but I tried to keep going.

"Maya Robinson. This project may look similar to the same volcano you've seen a million times before, but it is actually something different. I decided to investigate the ways that our emotions are connected to our physical reactions." I looked at the judges to see what *their* physical reactions were like. *When you're giving a presentation, always read the room,* my mom had said. The judge with the purse was listening intently, but the one with the cool necktie seemed distracted.

He looked at me apologetically. "Sorry, hon. I'm trying to listen, but we've been here since seven in the morning and I skipped breakfast. I need a snack."

"Oh, here!" The other judge pulled a granola bar out of her purse and tossed it to him lightly.

"Thanks, you're a lifesaver!" said Necktie Judge. "But careful, we need to set a good example for the kids," he joked. "Not too much throwing food. We wouldn't want a food fight."

As Necktie Judge was speaking, Marcus turned his amp back up even louder, and the end of the judge's sentence was lost to the guitar.

Giant Purse Judge frowned at the guitar noise. "What's that you said?"

Marcus turned it up even more, and I could see Principal Merriweather moving toward him from across the room, looking furious. Necktie Judge repeated himself, yelling at the top of his lungs.

"I SAID!" The screeching from the guitar continued.

"WE WOULDN'T!"

Principal Merriweather was waving her arms around, and Marcus was arguing with her.

"WANT! A! FOOD! FIGHT!"

At the exact same time as Necktie Judge finished his sentence, Principal Merriweather pulled the plug on the amp, ignoring Marcus's protests. The guitar went silent. Everyone turned to look at the screaming judge.

Everyone. Including Ralph.

WANT A FOOD FIGHT?

My eyes widened. Why was Ralph responding

without hearing his voice cue? And why was he reaching for Necktie Judge's granola bar?

"Oh no." It came out as a whisper. I'm pretty sure no one even heard me.

CHAPTER 16:
RESET BUTTON

And that's how my first science fair turned into a disaster. A pudding ... creamed corn ... disaster. And that's how Ralph and I ended up in the principal's office.

Principal Merriweather was in the middle of a world-class rant. Like, if she were in a movie she would probably get an Oscar for this. She didn't even seem to notice we were there anymore. She had a red pen in her hand, and she was waving it around like a sword of fury to punctuate her yelling. Every time she waved it, I imagined that she was making an exclamation point in the air.

"And another thing! Those grape juice stains! On the floor! Are probably never! Going to come out!

And the custodians! Are going to need overtime! To stay here late tonight and vacuum! Industrial wet-dry vac! And that's going to cost money! From the budget! This school is on a tight budget, Maya!"

When she got to that part, my eyes began to well up with tears. Seeing my project totally destroyed was one thing. A food fight mess was another. But what if I hurt the whole school? Were field trips and after-school programs going to be canceled because of me?

"Well, what do you have to say for yourself?" She stared at me expectantly. I was afraid that if I opened my mouth, I would start sobbing. I pressed my lips together and looked at the floor, ashamed.

Ralph, sitting next to me, seemed confused by the whole situation. I had never seen him confused before, but his eyes had turned blue. They were wide and round, and his mouth was turned down slightly. When he saw that I was about to cry, he reached over and patted me on the back.

MAYA IS SAD.

He looked up at Principal Merriweather, as if he

didn't understand why she didn't view this as an emergency.

MAYA IS SAD.

"And that's another thing! This robot! Surely you need some sort of . . . license or something for him. I'm going to tell your parents that I think he's a danger."

When she said that, I lost my composure. "No!" I cried out. "Not Ralph! He's not a danger! He's my friend!" I began to cry.

"Don't you raise your voice at me, young lady. My job is to look out for you and the other children of this school. Not to worry about robots. We don't even know what went wrong with him! What if that happens again? Why did he malfunction? Can you tell me that?"

I looked at the floor again, embarrassed to admit that I didn't know. I thought I had gotten so good with Ralph, that I understood how he worked. Maybe I had gotten overconfident. And the consequences were bad.

"This discussion is over." Principal Merriweather picked up the phone. To call who, I didn't know.

My parents? The police? Whoever comes and drags kids away when they get expelled from school? She began to dial.

I sat and watched her, not knowing what to say for myself and wishing there were a hole in the floor that I could crawl into and never come out of. My parents were going to be so angry at me, especially if they had to leave work in the middle of the day and come pick me up. I looked at Ralph. He looked down at me, apparently clueless about the destruction he had caused. Was he going to be taken apart and recycled? If he was, it would be my fault. The proof of Christopher's hard work, his brilliance, gone. For nothing. And it would be on me, for bringing Ralph to school and putting him in an unfamiliar situation. He had been a good friend to me, and this is how I repaid him. By ruining everything.

I leaned against Ralph and closed my eyes. I wanted to make a wish, but I didn't even know what to wish for. Instead, I cried, and for once I didn't even think to be embarrassed about it.

Just then, there was a small crash. *What now?* I opened my eyes.

"Principal Merriweather! Wait!"

Jada and MJ had burst into the office, pushing the door so hard that it smashed against the wall. They were followed closely by Ms. Montgomery, and ... Elijah? MJ did a double take when he noticed the damage done by the doorknob. "Oops. Sorry," he said sheepishly.

"Principal Merriweather, I'm sorry," Ms. Montgomery said. She was out of breath, as though she had been chasing them. "I tried to tell them you were—"

"It's not Maya's fault!" interrupted Jada. "I don't mean to interrupt, but this is important! The food fight. It's not her fault."

Principal Merriweather narrowed her eyes at them and slowly lowered the telephone. "And whose fault was it, then?"

Elijah was fiddling nervously with a pencil. He looked like he did *not* want to be in the principal's office, even if he wasn't the one in trouble. MJ, who was panting and leaning against a chair for support, looked up at him and nodded supportively. "Tell her, bro."

Elijah stepped forward and swallowed hard

before speaking. "Zoe Winters. I saw her messing around with the robot before the fair started. She opened up his back, and she was messing with stuff and pressing things."

Principal Merriweather and Ms. Montgomery looked at me. "Is this true?"

Zoe? But when could she have . . . ?

I gasped. "The water. She told me to go get some water before the fair. That's why she was being so nice to me. She was trying to get me out of the way so she could mess around with Ralph."

Principal Merriweather nodded thoughtfully. "Ms. Montgomery, do me a favor. Go and fetch Ms. Winters and let's see what she has to say about this." Ms. Montgomery nodded and stepped out of the room.

I swallowed, closed my eyes for a second, and took a deep breath. This time, when I spoke, I went slowly and chose my words with care. I had to make it count.

I looked at Principal Merriweather and tried to use my most grown-up voice. "Principal Merriweather, you asked me what went wrong and why Ralph malfunctioned. He usually has a special voice command keyword. He's not supposed to do something unless you tell him to do it. Like a smart phone. So normally, saying 'throw food' should not make him throw food. That would be very inconvenient, if you think about it. He's never done anything like that before." I turned to Ralph. "Ralph, what's the status of your voice command function?"

VOICE COMMAND KEYWORD DISENGAGED.

"How did it get disengaged?"

ON SYSTEM RESET, NEW VOICE COMMAND REQUIRED.

System reset?! Zoe must have turned Ralph off and back on. Without me there to re-establish the voice command, he must have gone haywire—especially in a noisy cafeteria with lots of loud voices chattering at once. "What time did system reset happen?"

LAST SYSTEM RESET OCCURRED AT EIGHT FIFTY-EIGHT A.M.

But how did she even do that? "Ralph, turn around." I examined his back, where the carefully concealed access panel was. There were harsh scratches around the panel, as though someone who didn't know how the latch worked had tried to pry it open it with keys or a pen or something sharp. "Look at this! Look what she did to him! This is horrible!"

A small voice behind me said, "Well, it doesn't look that bad."

I looked up to see Zoe standing in the door. Without warning, a hot rage filled my whole body, and I started to fling myself at her, fists out. "You did this! Look what you did to my friend! You hurt him!"

Jada and MJ each grabbed one of my arms. "It's not worth it, Maya," MJ hissed into my ear. "Let her be. She knows what she did."

"She hurt Ralph for no reason! She's always bothering me, and she was mad that I had a friend." I gave up fighting MJ and Jada and slumped into their arms, defeated. "She wanted to hurt me. So she hurt Ralph."

Principal Merriweather pointed her red pen at Zoe. "Is that the case, Zoe?"

Zoe looked around the room, searching for something to say. "I . . . I thought it had games on it." The lie was so weak that Ms. Montgomery openly rolled her eyes and Jada let out a loud *pfffft* noise. I snorted.

"Ha!" said MJ. "If that ain't the biggest lie I ever—" Principal Merriweather held up a hand, and he stopped.

"Zoe, please spare us. No need to insult our intelligence. Why did you do this?"

Zoe looked at me, then looked at the floor.

When she looked back up, her eyes were red. "Maya is so good at science, and she's always talking about the book she finished reading or the movie she watched. She thinks she's too cool for everyone. I thought that this year since she wasn't glued to her other two friends for once, and we were in the same class, maybe she and I could be friends." She sniffled. "But she just . . . She ignores me! She'll even talk to the new kid! But not to me!" Now she was full-on wailing.

I was stunned.

"Zoe . . . if you wanted to be my friend . . . you could have said hi. Or something."

Elijah tilted his head to one side. "Just so you know, she wouldn't *really* talk to me, either."

Man. I guess I had been . . . not the best to Elijah.

That's not how I was taught to treat someone who was new and needed a friend. I looked up at him and whispered, "I'm sorry, Elijah. I have a hard time with . . ." I didn't know how to end the sentence. "Friend. Stuff."

He smiled. "It's okay. But Zoe, why didn't you just say hi, like she said? I at least tried that."

Zoe sniffled again and looked at both of us with her mouth open, but no words came out. Then she furrowed her eyebrows. "I don't know! I guess . . . I guess . . ." She trailed off and wiped her nose on her sleeve.

Everyone looked around the room awkwardly, avoiding eye contact, until Jada spoke up.

"Maybe it was just hard," she said. She looked around the room, then directly at Zoe. She repeated herself. "Maybe it was just hard. To say hi."

Zoe nodded. I looked at her, listening to her quiet sniffles and not knowing what to say to her. Principal Merriweather cleared her throat.

"Okay. Zoe, it seems you and I need to have a conversation," said Principal Merriweather. "Maya, are you able to fix your robot?"

"I should be able to," I said.

I looked at Ralph, and he looked back at me, waiting for instructions. "Ralph, re-engage voice command. Set keyword to 'Ralph.' Set my voice as primary user."

VOICE COMMAND KEYWORD RE-ENGAGED.

"And we owe everyone an apology, Ralph. It was an accident, but we made a really big mess. Ralph, please apologize."

Ralph stood up from his seat. It took him a second, since he wasn't used to sitting down, and he bent his knees and stretched them carefully as he figured out the process of standing back up. He turned his metal bucket head left and right, looking around the room. He put his hands behind his back politely.

I AM VERY SORRY ABOUT THE MESS. MAYA IS SORRY TOO. MAYA IS SAD. WE ARE SORRY.

Principal Merriweather actually smiled. "You're forgiven, Ralph. Now, everyone out of my office." We all headed to the door, including Zoe.

"Oh, Ms. Winters, not you. We need to chat."

As Principal Merriweather was shutting the door behind them, I caught a last view of Zoe. She looked close to tears again. I said the only thing I could think to say. "Hey. It's going to be okay," I told her. She looked startled, then nodded. The door closed.

The rest of us stepped into the hallway. Jada and MJ each put an arm around me, and Ralph put his hand on my back. And I wanted to feel better, I really did.

But now I had no science fair project at all. It was wrecked. I was going to get an F. And Zoe getting in trouble would do nothing to change that.

CHAPTER 17:
A REAL SCIENTIST

I slowly made my way from the principal's office back into the cafeteria, followed by Jada, MJ, Ralph, Elijah, and Ms. Montgomery. Somehow, in the time we were gone, things had sort of gone back to normal. There was still a mess everywhere, but the kids who didn't get taken to the nurse for catching a glob of pudding in the eye were back at their stations, and the judges were moving from place to place, carefully stepping over creamed corn.

"The show must go on," said Ms. Montgomery. "I'm going to walk around and see who needs assistance. Maya, why don't you go clean up your station before those mashed potatoes start to get crusty."

Ew.

"Jada and I can help you," said MJ.

Elijah cleared his throat. "If it's okay with you guys, I'm gonna go back and clean off my table."

"Sure," said Jada. "Thanks again for telling us what happened."

"No problem," said Elijah. He paused a moment. "Maybe sometime we can all . . . talk? Or something."

"Yeah," I said. "Or we can hang out? Do you . . . By any chance have you seen Star Wars, Elijah? If not, we can try to get you caught up."

He grinned an enormous grin. "Try? Try? As a great Jedi once said: Do, or do not. There is no try." He waved over his shoulder as he walked away. "Catch y'all later."

We made our way over to where my book bag and my project were. My table had turned into a mashed potato cemetery, complete with crusty mashed potato zombies starting to harden and smell weird. It was as gross as that sounds. Jada grabbed a roll of paper towels from a neighboring table and handed a huge handful to each of us.

"Well," she said, wiping the table, "I think we can

still say . . . this is the worst science fair ever."

The three of us laughed. Ralph smiled even though it was clear he didn't fully get the joke. It felt so good to laugh with my friends again.

"Thanks, you guys," I said. "For having my back."

"We always got you, Maya," said MJ, shooting a crumpled-up paper towel into a nearby garbage can. He missed. Jada shook her head as he went to pick it up.

"Terrible," she said. "That boy still ain't got no jump shot." She turned to me. "Maya, he's right. We got your back. But why didn't you tell us about, um . . ." She waved her arms at Ralph and said in an exaggerated dramatic voice, "You know, the fact that you constructed a FULLY FUNCTIONAL ROBOT? And y'all were just chillin'? You couldn't invite us over? What's that about? Ralph, what's that about, man?"

I DO NOT KNOW WHAT THAT IS ABOUT.

I sighed. "I dunno. I didn't even do it by myself. It's kind of a long story."

MJ started to shoot another paper towel basketball toward the trash, then thought better of it and walked over to throw it away. "We love long stories," he said.

"I know. And I don't know why I didn't tell you. I wasn't trying to keep him a secret. But this year has been, you know, different."

Jada stopped wiping the table and frowned. "Different how?"

"Well, you guys are in the same class and I'm not, and you have these cool new friends and a new teacher, and my teacher is mean and Zoe has been mean to me, and I didn't make any new friends, and you don't need me." Everything came pouring out at once. The hot feeling was coming over my face again, and a tear escaped despite my best efforts. I wiped it away quickly. "You have a whole other life."

MJ and Jada glanced at each other, then back at me. They both looked heartbroken. Jada leaned over and gave me a quick hug. "Maya . . . you're my *girl*. From day one. You think we wouldn't be friends anymore because we're in a different class? That can't stop us!"

"Yeah," said MJ. "We thought *you* were busy

because it seemed like you didn't want to talk or hang anymore. We been out of the loop."

"We're always gonna be friends," said Jada. "Three Jedi Knights, no matter what. High school, college, doesn't matter. And if we pick up some new musketeers along the way, it sure can't hurt. Right, Ralphie boy?" She knocked on his metal torso, which emitted a cheery *clang clang*.

"Ugh," I said, walking around behind Ralph and looking at his scratched-up panel again. "I can't believe she did this. Look at him! She messed him up. Ralph, does it hurt?"

IT DOES NOT HURT, MAYA. I AM MESSED UP BUT NOT ON THE INSIDE.

MJ laughed. "This guy is a poet." He leaned in and peered at Ralph's scratches. "You know, Maya, I bet my dad can fix this in the auto shop. It's not too different from scratches on a car. He can buff it out. And I'm sure he'll give you the family and friends discount."

"MJ, you know I don't have money for that."

"Sure you do. The discount is a hundred percent off. And maybe you and Ralph can help out around the shop or something."

I smiled. "Thanks, bro."

MJ ran a finger over the scratched metal. "Maybe this weekend y'all can come over and we can fix Ralph's back and then we can watch the basketball game or something. Or play video games. Maybe invite that Elijah kid if you want, Maya."

"Good idea. And Maya can show us all the cool stuff Ralph can do," Jada chimed in. "You know, other than throwing pudding at Zoe's head." She burst out laughing. "Oh, man. That image is gonna be with me for a long, long time."

I laughed, too. "Ralph, do you want to hang out with my friends this weekend?"

I WANT TO HANG OUT WITH YOUR FRIENDS THIS WEEKEND, MAYA. THAT SOUNDS REALLY FUN.

"Then it's a date," I said. "Assuming I don't have to stay in school this weekend mopping the floor and scrubbing the walls." I scraped at a particularly nasty bit of drying mashed potatoes on the corner of the table. Jada, MJ, and Ralph fell silent, each of them getting into a rhythm of wiping and scraping and washing, and for a moment we were quiet together.

I was deep into my cleaning zone, trying to use the tip of a pencil to get some pudding out of the zipper of my book bag, when I heard a small, hesitant voice behind me.

"Excuse me?"

I turned around, startled. It was a tiny girl, a first grader I recognized from seeing her on the playground in the morning sometimes. She had pink beads in her hair, and she was wearing a T-shirt that said NASA on it. She was holding a small notebook and a pencil. She looked up at me with huge eyes.

I gave her a small wave. "Hi. Um . . . can I help you?"

She waved back. "Can you explain your science fair project?"

My face fell. "Well, actually, I don't have one. A project. I mean, I had one, but it got ruined. Sorry. Nothing to see here, I guess. I'm sure someone else has a cool project that you could check out."

The little girl looked confused. She pointed at Ralph. "Your robot. He's right there. Can you explain how he works?"

"Oh. He's not my science fai–"

MJ swatted at me with a paper towel. "Maya, quit tripping and tell her how the robot works. The kid wants to hear about the robot, tell her about the robot."

"Give the people what they want!" exclaimed Jada. "Ralph, tell Maya to give the people what they want!"

MAYA, GIVE THE PEOPLE WHAT THEY WANT!

"Okay, okay!" I said. I turned to the girl. "Um, I don't really have a presentation prepared."

"I wanna know how he works," she said. She held up her pencil and notebook eagerly.

I fiddled with my hands. I had practiced the other presentation for so long. Now I was supposed to make something up off the top of my head?

Then, in the back of my mind, I remembered Mr. Mac's speech. *Use your gifts to help others.* I straightened my back and took a deep breath. When I spoke again, I tried to muster up the most confident voice I could.

"This is Ralph," I began. "He is a personal assistance robot. He was designed by Christopher MacMillan, a robotics engineering student at Stanford University." The girl was scribbling in her notepad. I peeked and saw that she wasn't really writing words, but drawing a picture of Ralph. Suddenly, I felt stronger.

I cleared my throat and spoke up more loudly. "I used Christopher's notes to make Ralph fully operational, and I have a prototype of a unique kind of battery that he needs to work. Ralph can provide support with household tasks, such as dishes and cleaning. He also has a number of notable features that make him unique."

A few other kids had gathered around, and they

stood listening attentively. I kept going. "If you'll look carefully at Ralph's mouth, you'll see that it is made of a series of LED lights. They can move in different patterns and colors to help Ralph make facial expressions. He also responds to voice commands. Ralph, say hello to everyone."

HELLO TO EVERYONE.

The kids squealed and laughed in delight. Other people, hearing the commotion, drifted over. Suddenly I was speaking to a small crowd. I lifted my voice even higher.

"Notice that Ralph has special feet. They have tire treads, which allow him to roll over rough surfaces. But they also have joints and actuators— little motors that help him to bend and move his legs the way we do. Ralph, march in place and then show everyone how you can jump." Ralph did as I asked, marching and then jumping straight into the air and landing gracefully. Everyone in the crowd gasped and clapped.

I kept talking. I talked about the triple-Z battery, Ralph's ability to learn new ways to communicate and adapt his language, what bioinspiration is, the research of Dr. Jacqueline Yazzie. I talked and talked and talked. After a while, I realized that it didn't even feel like I was making a presentation. I was sharing information on something I knew well. When I was finally done, I glanced at the clock in the corner and realized I had been talking for fifteen minutes straight.

"So. That's how Ralph works. He is a robot, but he's also my friend. Um."

How are you supposed to end a presentation? "The end."

Jada leaned over and whispered in my ear. *"Ask them if they have any questions."*

Oh, yeah. "Does . . . Does anyone have any questions?"

The crowd applauded. I didn't realize that I had been holding my breath, but suddenly I exhaled and it was like a whole hurricane leaving my body. MJ stepped up to the front, clasping his hands professionally. "Thank you, thank you, everyone! If there are no questions, Maya needs a break now. Please enjoy the rest of the science fair, and have a great day."

Everyone began to scatter, wandering off to see the rest of the projects. A bunch of tall eighth graders had been standing at the back of the crowd, and they walked away, talking cheerily. As they stepped aside, I could see that someone had been standing behind them, beyond my view. The person stepped forward. My heart dropped.

It was Ms. Rodríguez.

"Hello, Ms. Robinson. I think we need to talk about your science fair project."

She sauntered up, looking at the table. We had made good progress on cleaning it, but my volcano was still ruined.

"I know," I said slowly. "I had one, and I worked hard on it, but it got ruined. And I know it's a huge part of my grade." I was gonna fail science. My favorite class.

Ms. Rodríguez smiled a rare smile. "Two things, Ms. Robinson. First of all, I did not know that you preferred to be called Maya. I apologize. Should I call you that from now on?"

Well, I didn't see that coming. I nodded wordlessly.

"And secondly, I would suggest that this"—she gestured at Ralph—"this *companion* of yours . . . well, your work with him ought to count for your science fair project. While the robot's design comes from someone else, it is clear that you have conducted independent research. You have used trial and error. You have pursued your curiosity. So if it's okay with you, I will go ahead and mark this presentation down as your official science fair project entry."

My eyes went wide. "Oh my gosh! Yes, please. Thank you. Thank you so much."

Ms. Rodríguez nodded. "My pleasure. Please keep up the good work." She looked me up and down. "And you have mashed potatoes on your shirt."

"Oh!" I looked down at my shirt. Yuck. When I looked back up, she was gone. And Ralph was holding out a wet paper towel. I took it and smiled at him. As I was wiping, poking, and scraping at the white lump on my shirt, I felt a tap on my knee. I looked down. It was the little girl with the NASA shirt. She looked up at me.

"I had a question, but I didn't get to ask."

I knelt down, facing her. "Oh, I'm so sorry. What was it?"

She held up her pencil. "What is your name? And are you a real scientist?"

I looked down at her, then back at MJ and Jada, who were grinning behind me. I looked at Ralph, whose eyes were shining bright and green. And then I answered.

"My name is Maya Robinson. And yes, I am a real scientist."

ACKNOWLEDGMENTS

As Mariame Kaba once said, "Everything worthwhile is done with other people." There are so many people whose love and support made this book possible. I couldn't possibly name them all, but I do want to tell you about a few of them!

Thank you to my husband, the kind of supportive cheerleader that every writer dreams of. Thank you to my whole family, and the people I grew up with, many of whom planted seeds in my mind that grew into the characters in this book. Thank you especially to my niece. Maya was born the moment you looked out the window and said, "I just wish I could have a robot who could go everywhere with me and be my best friend."

Thanks to my phenomenal agent, Chris Parris-

Lamb, who believed in this story from the start. Thanks to the whole editorial team at Kokila that brought it to life, especially Namrata Tripathi and Zareen Jaffery.

I'm grateful to my dear friend Stephany Cuevas for her translation assistance, to Payton A. Boateng for her editorial assistance, and to Leah Castleberry for consulting me on matters of artificial intelligence and robotics.

When I was trying to finish a first draft of this manuscript, Jeny and Gil Mathis graciously opened their home to me so that I could have a place to get away and write—thank you!

In addition to being a writer, I began my professional career as a middle-school science teacher. I got to spend time with so many brilliant students who loved science and who brought many diverse gifts to our classroom. To all of my former students and fellow educators—thank you for inspiring me with your energy, wit, creativity, and kindness.